STANTON BLISS

STANTON
Bliss

T L SWAN

This book is a work of fiction. Any resemblances to actual persons, living or dead, events, or locales are purely coincidental.

ACKNOWLEDGEMENTS

It takes a team to write a book.

I am one of the lucky ones and my precious team has grown with each one I have written.

Let me start my thank you's.

Mum, You are the best.......that is all!

Vicki, you have been with me for ten years before I wrote one word. Your friendship and advice on my writing mean more to me than you could ever know. Thank you for every thing that you do for me and please know that you are stuck with me for life........you can not escape.

Amanda, my loveable sarcastic Dom. I met you through Adore as a reader and never in a million years did I expect for you to become one of my closest friends. Thank you for everything that you do, you are so very appreciated.

Rachel, the funniest and sweetest chick on this earth. You live on the other side of the world from me and yet I feel like I have known you forever. The day your blog asked you to review Adore was a huge blessing in my life. I can never ever repay you and Amanda for all that you do for me. If it wasn't for you two I probably would have sold one book to date.

Lisa, funny, sweet and totally addicted to Joshua. Your friendship brightens my days, another blogger turned beautiful friend. Thank you for making me laugh, I truly value our friendship.

Anissa, I honestly didn't know that girls like you existed. You are the sweetest, kindest person I have been lucky enough to meet. It was your blog (The Christian Grey Fan Page) that started me off. I can never thank you enough and its not even about books any more between us, its about friendship.

Linda, you are kicking my ass all the way home and I love you for it. Thank you for all that you do for me.

Victoria, my smart little friend and an awesome author, thank you for all that you do for me.

To my beta team. Tara, Nadia, Charlotte, Anne, Sharon, Renee, Brooke, Tracey, Laura, Donna, Rachel, Nicole, Laura, Kelli, Nikki. Thank you girls, you make me better. I couldn't do this without you.

To the awesome girls in my street team The Lamborghini Chicks....... oh my god, you blow my mind with your support. Thank you so much for everything that you do.

To the beloved girls in the Swan Squad.......I LOVE YOU.......you make my days brighter, thank you for your friendship and giving me a safe place to hang out. I am forever grateful and sincerely hope that one day we can all meet.

To all the wonderful bloggers in the world, your support has helped me more than you could ever know. Special mention to Three Chicks and Their Books, Christian Grey Fan Page, The Rock stars of Romance, Sassy Savvy and Fabulous, Book Lovers Down Under and Sharing The Book Love

My beautiful husband and my gorgeous kids, you are my everything.

I love you more than life itself.

And YOU. Every single person who has purchased Stanton. I still pinch myself that people actually read my books, let alone enjoy them.

Thank you, thank you, thank you.

And Last but not least I would like to thank my beautiful Joshua and Natasha. You came to me at a time when I didn't think this was possible. You did not go away and you never left me......every time I thought I can't do this, you whispered yes you can, keep going. You got this.

Although it was me who wrote your story, I think it was you who really wrote mine.

I miss you already.

GRATITUDE

*The quality of being thankful; readiness to show
appreciation for and to return kindness.*

CHAPTER 1

REGRETS. FOR EVERY single minute of every hour that I sat locked in that room, I had a new regret. Regret that I didn't love him sooner. Regret that I had wasted so much time being insecure and unsure. Regret that I blamed myself so hard for my beloved father's death. But when it all comes down to it, the only person who feels the pain of my regrets is me. Nobody gives a flying fuck how insecure I am on the inside, so why did I put myself through it for so long?

I've been given a second chance at my life.

A do-over.

I'm going to take the bastard by both horns and ride it home hard, without fear, without hesitation and without one more single regret.

Look out world. Here I come!

We arrived in Thailand this afternoon and I am in Kamala surrounded by my loved ones. The sun is setting over the horizon and the staff are lighting the candles that are scattered throughout the garden. Joshua and his family are here along with Adrian, Nicholas and Abbie, and my family. We are sitting around the pool area of the main house after enjoying a beautiful meal, it's been a big day... a big month, actually. Exhausted doesn't even come close to how I'm feeling, but the very last thing that I want to do is go to bed. I don't want to miss one single second with these beautiful people. I've missed them all so much and family has never been more important. Didge, Abbie and I are in the pool and we have swum to the other end to talk in private.

On the steps of the pool, in the darkness, we talk quietly. We haven't had a moment to ourselves since I was found two days ago.

"I've missed you two," I breathe. I can't believe I'm actually here with them.

Abbie smiles and wraps her arms around Bridge and I as we sit on either side of her.

"Tell me, what exactly have I missed?" I whisper.

"A lot of crying."

I smile sadly.

"Nothing has happened since you left, Tash. Our whole world stopped."

My eyes flick to my beautiful man who is sitting opposite Nicholas on a deckchair at the other end of the pool. He is writing in a notepad the requirements for tomorrow's wedding. Glancing up, he catches me watching him and smiles sexily.

"How was Joshua?"

The girls exchange looks.

"When I was missing and he thought I was dead, how was he?" I ask again.

"He was..." Abbie screws up her face and stops to articulate her wording.

"I can imagine he was a raging lunatic," I add as my eyes flick back to him.

The girls both exchange looks and shake their head. "No."

I frown. "What do you mean?"

"He was different."

"How so?"

"He withdrew and became a recluse."

My heart drops and my eyes find him again as I deepen my frown.

"He was too broken to be angry," Bridget whispers sadly.

"Oh." I sit and think for a moment. "He wasn't going berserk like a maniac?" I ask. I don't believe this – I thought he would have been raging like a bull.

The girls both shake their heads. "No, he would have been easier to handle if he acted how we all thought he was going to."

"He hardly spoke," Abbie whispers.

I sigh. My beautiful man has been through so much.

"He just gave up," Bridget says sadly.

We all sit and look straight ahead, lost in our own thoughts.

"Adrian was probably the strongest."

"Adrian?" I smirk. This *is* unexpected.

The girls both smile. "He was awesome. He ran the company and organised the press releases, not to mention how much he was trying to keep everyone calm."

I smile and our eyes flick to Adrian as he sits with Mum. He is being all animated, telling her a story, and she is laughing out loud.

"Is he back with Nicholas?" I ask.

"No, Nicholas just came to help him."

My eyes drop to the dark water. God, they have all been through so much. I need to talk to Joshua. "How did Adrian and Cameron find me?" I forgot to ask this question before now.

"It was Adrian. He heard Amelie call you Cinderella."

My mouth drops open in shock. "You're kidding?"

Bridget shakes her head. "Nope, she was at the jail visiting Joshua and she said something in the waiting room about Joshua never being suited to Cinderella. Adrian caught on and then they all followed her to the house."

I put my hand over my mouth. "Oh my God." I frown, my stupid plan actually worked.

"They staked out her house and she was walking around in the rain with a gun looking for you in the forest."

My stomach turns at the memory of the heavy rain on the tin roof, that horrific sound will haunt me forever. A vision of her dead body lying in the rain flashes through my mind and a cold shiver runs through me.

"It was like fucking James Bond shit." Abbie shakes her head in disbelief.

"More like Quentin Tarantino," I whisper.

Abbie nods. "That, too."

"How often did Amelie visit Joshua in prison?" I ask. I bet she was trying to slime her way in. How dare she visit him in prison when it was her that put him there?

Abbie shrugs. "I think that was the first time. She didn't even get to see him because she got a call and ran out, that's when the boys followed her back to the house where you were being kept."

I narrow my eyes deep in thought. "So, she got a call and ran out?"

"I think so," Sighs Bridget.

"It must have been when they realised I had escaped."

The girls both nod in agreement. "Probably."

Holy hell, what a fuck up. My mind drifts to Amelie. On one hand, I feel bad for what I have done, and yet I feel a venom in my bloodstream that I have never had before. How could she have done this to Joshua? Her love and my love for him were so different. I gave him away to give him time to pursue her because I thought that's what would make him really happy, and yet she would rather he be dead than with me.

He could have died. I nearly *did* die. My eyes drift down to the horrible, thick purple scar on my wrist.

I hate her. I hate every damn thing about that poisonous bitch. My gaze wanders to Joshua again, and when our eyes meet, he seems to read my mind, and frowns in question.

I shake my head softly in a dismissive gesture and smile.

"I'm going to go see my man," I whisper.

I swim up to his end of the pool along with the girls. I'm looking forward to getting him to myself tonight. Mum and Bridget have been by my side constantly since my release, understandably scared to take their eyes off of me.

"You ready for bed, Presh?" he asks.

I smile. That name will never get old.

"Hey. You two are not supposed to be sleeping together on the night before the wedding," Bridget announces.

Joshua looks at her deadpan. "Yeah, well, that's not happening."

I nod my weary head and swim over to the stairs. Joshua retrieves a towel and wraps me in it protectively as I climb out. I kiss his chest through his t-shirt. It's so damn good to be home and in his arms.

"Take me to bed, my Lamborghini," I whisper.

"We're turning in," Joshua announces to our families.

"Its only ten." Cameron frowns as he stands on the pool stairs. We are obviously interrupting his impending swim.

"Yes, so? Go and swim in your pool and get out of mine." Joshua yawns.

Everyone smiles and stands. "See you tomorrow. Bye." They all call out as they start to head back to their rooms. The girls are staying in the house next door, the boys in the one after that, and then the bodyguards in the end house. Margaret and Robert are staying in a luxury resort down the hill.

Suddenly alone with my man, I stand with my arms wrapped around him and I look up at his beautiful face.

He smiles and kisses me gently on the lips. "You ready for bed, my bride to be?"

"Mrs. Stanton?" I whisper. Is this real? Are we really getting married tomorrow?

He smiles the sexiest damn smile I have ever seen.

"Sounds old." I smirk.

"Sounds good," he whispers. "And old."

I narrow my eyes. "You are older than me, you do remember that don't you, Mr. Stanton?"

He kisses me again, and his tongue sweeps gently through my open mouth, making me feel a throb that only he can ever instil.

"I feel ninety," he whispers.

I giggle. "Well, you best get Cam to write you a script for Viagra, because I am feeling seventeen and dangerous."

I wake to the bed bouncing, and force myself to pry my heavy eyelids open. Mum, Bridget and Abbie are sitting on the end of the bed with stupid grins on their faces.

"Wake up, sleepy head." Mum smiles.

I sit up in a rush as I remember what today is. *Holy crap.* "Where's Joshua?" I stammer.

Bridget rolls her eyes, adding in a soft shake of her head. "He's on wedding crack or something."

I smile broadly. "What's he doing?"

"He has been ordering everyone around like a lunatic since 6:00 a.m. this morning. He has poor Cameron up a tree stringing fairy lights, Adrian in charge of flowers, and Nicholas making playlists. Ben is in charge of the tables and chairs, and he has Brock in charge of the food.

Abbie rolls her eyes. "And that's just stupid because we all know that Brock will just eat all of the food."

I smirk. "Sounds dreadful."

"It's good to be a girl today." Mum smiles

"Where's Max?"

"He is helping Ben."

I flop back down onto my pillow. "This is, like, my favourite day ever." I smile in delight. "What time are we getting married?"

"Five o'clock."

"On the ledge, right?"

"Yes."

"What do they want us to do?" I ask.

"Nothing. Just show up, I imagine." Mum smirks.

I smile broadly before jumping out of bed and running to the bathroom as the girls lay on my bed. This is it! This is the day I have been waiting for forever. I can hardly contain my excitement. That is, until I take a long, hard look at myself in the mirror. Holy crap, this just won't do. I look like death and I'm pasty white. I march back out to the girls and put my hand on my hip in disgust.

"That's it, we are going to the beach."

The girls all look at me like I've gone completely mad. "You want to go the beach? Today?"

"I look like freaking Casper the Ghost. I need some sun, stat."

Abbie bites her bottom lip to stifle her smile. "There's my girl. I've missed my drama queen."

I smile, take out my phone, dial my favourite number – Lambo – and he answers first ring. A rush of excitement runs through me that I can just ring him whenever I want now.

"Good morning, my Presh."

I smile as an overwhelming feeling of love fills me. "Good morning."

"Are you ok?" he asks gently.

"Perfect," I breathe. "Do you want me to do anything?" I ask.

"No. I've got it. Spend the day pampering yourself. Get a massage or whatever girls do on their wedding day."

My heart melts. "You know I love you, right?"

I can hear him smile through the phone. "You better."

"I want to go to the beach," I announce.

"What?"

"I want to get some sun."

He hesitates. "Ah, Presh, I have a lot to do and I don't want to be worrying about you being safe."

"Joshua."

"Yes." He sighs.

"I'm going to go to the beach with the girls and I will take Max." My eyes flicker to the girls who are all smirking as they listen.

He hesitates again as he thinks, and I know he wants to stop me, but also doesn't want to upset me today.

"Tash," he whispers.

"Joshua, I have been locked in a room for a really long time and I want to feel the sun and salt on my skin on my wedding day. We will only be three hours."

I hear him inhale deeply in frustration as he thinks for a moment. "Fine." He sighs. "But you are taking Brock, Max and Peter."

I smile. That was easier than I thought it would be. "Ok."

"Three hours."

"Yes, boss."

"I mean it, or I'm coming to get you myself."

"I will meet you on the ledge at five?" I ask hopefully.

I feel him smile again. "Try and stop me."

Joshua

I hang up the phone and roll my eyes. Fucking hell. The beach! I walk over to the trees that Cameron, Brock and Max are discussing.

"They should go from this one to this one." Cameron points to a branch. "Not that one to this one."

Brock shakes his head in disgust as he stands looking up at the trees with both hands on his hips. "You are an idiot. They don't go that way. When it's dark, it is supposed to be all over, not in a line. It isn't a fucking Christmas tree, you know."

Max rolls his eyes in frustration at Cameron who obviously has no idea what he is talking about.

"I did this for the engagement and I nailed it. I know what I'm doing," Cameron replies dryly.

I smirk at the shit they are carrying on with. "So, Natasha wants to go to the beach."

Max's eyes shoot up to me, and he frowns.

I nod. "I know."

"Tell her we are too fucking busy to play Gidget for fucks sake!" Cameron snaps in frustration as he begins to pull the lights from the box.

"Brock and Max can you take her?" I reply.

Brock smiles broadly and high-fives Max. "We are so out of here."

"Thank God," Max mutters.

Cameron looks at me deadpan. "Oh, great, so I'm doing all this fucking shit on my own now?"

"No, Murph and I are here to help." I smirk.

"Where is Ben?" Cameron snaps.

"He's going, too."

Brock and Max snicker under their breaths.

"This is Bullshit. Why aren't Abbie and Didge helping us with this crap?"

"They are going to the beach."

Cameron shakes his head as he starts to re-climb the tree. "If I ever get married, Stan, you are going to pay, and I'm going to the beach while you do all this shit."

I smile and turn my attention to Brock. "Don't let her out of your sight."

"I won't."

"Not for even a second," I warn.

"I know, I know. Relax."

Brock and I have somehow turned a corner, It turns out Tash

was right and perhaps we do have a lot in common after all. He was there for me in my darkest of days, even visiting me in prison. His support means a lot to Tash, therefore it means a lot to me, too. I turn my attention to Max.

"Max?"

His eyes meet mine. "Yes."

"You won't be working tonight."

His face falls. "Oh," he mutters, sounding dejected.

"I want you at the wedding as a guest, a friend of ours."

He drops his head and smiles at the ground.

"And I also want to thank you."

He looks up and frowns. "For what?"

"For staying by Natasha's side when she needed you the most."

He smiles a relieved smile and Ben slaps him on the back.

"Getting pathetic now, Stanton?" Brock questions, as he raises a brow.

I look at him straight faced "Don't make me hurt you, Marx."

"As if." He shakes his head as he and Max start to walk up the stone stairs that hug the cliff.

"Three hours!" I call after them.

"Yes," They both reply in a bored voice.

"And don't let her out of your sight," I repeat.

They ignore me and keep walking.

My attention turns to Cameron who is now up the ladder, he looks down at me and shakes his head. "There is no way in Hell they will be back in three hours."

I shake my head in defeat. "Tell me something I don't already know."

I slowly button up my white, crisp shirt as I look in the mirror.

Its my wedding day.

A day I thought had been stolen forever.

She's back.

I drop my head and smile.

My girl is back, along with my appetite, my sex drive and my freedom.

"Stop fucking smiling. You're getting all creepy?" Cameron tuts from his place next to me as he pulls up his pants.

I throw him a wink and smile broadly again.

"Photo time," Murph states as he starts to snap photos with his camera. Cameron grabs his crotch and sticks out his tongue while Ben smirks from his place at the end of the bed.

Adrian drops the camera. "I don't have my magnifying glass on the camera. You idiot. Put it away," he replies dryly.

Cameron shrugs. "Like you would need to zoom to see this lizard. It's a beast." He grabs his crotch again and shakes it.

I roll my eyes as Adrian screws up his face in disgust. "God, you're an animal. Who calls their dick a Lizard beast?"

Cameron shrugs again. "If the shoe fits."

"You're a tool," Ben mutters under his breath, shaking his head.

Cameron rearranges his tie in the mirror next to me while I pull up my pants.

"You need to hurry," Adrian snaps. He has been ready for over an hour. We are in the second house and Natasha and the girls are in the main house.

I do up my fly and the pants fall straight down over my hips, causing Adrian's face falls in horror. He holds his hands up in a stop sign. "Oh my fucking God! Tell me those pants fit you?"

"Shit." I pull them up again and they fall straight back down. I've lost a lot of weight.

Adrian puts both of his hands on his cheeks in horror as his eyes widen. "Do we have a fucking belt?"

I turn and walk into Adrian's wardrobe and look around.

"I don't have one!" Adrian shrieks as his eyes flicker around to the boys. "Do you have one? Cameron, Ben, does anyone have a belt?"

I shrug. "Maybe in my wardrobe in the other house, I don't know. I'm usually in board shorts the whole time I'm here. I've never needed one before."

Adrian runs his hands through his hair in a panic before he looks at his watch. "This is a disaster. Ben, can you go next door and find us a belt, please?" He looks like he's about to hyperventilate and Ben disappears out of the room.

Dad walks into the room with Wilson and Scott, handing us all a beer.

"A toast." He smiles.

My heart rate instantly rises and I'm so grateful that I have him here with me today.

"To the unbreakable Stantons," he announces proudly.

Four words are all it takes to bring a lump to my throat. Four small words that mean more to me than he will ever know. I recited them repeatedly to myself in prison on the day Natasha and I were originally supposed to get married.

They saved my life.

"To the unbreakable Stantons," we echo as we clink our bottles together.

I smile as he wraps his arms around me and gives me a strong hug and a kiss on the cheek.

"I'm proud of you, son."

I nod and smile as emotion steals my words.

Ben re-enters the room and shakes his head.

Adrian's eyes widen in horror. "What?" he snaps.

"No belt."

"This is my worst nightmare," he whispers.

I smile at the floor and raise a brow. Give me a break. Not having a belt is far from my nightmares.

My eyes glance up to the stone staircase for the hundredth time as my heart hammers in my chest.

"She changed her mind," Cameron whispers. "Smart woman. She's currently on her way to Ibiza."

I throw him a glare and Adrian chuckles.

Eight years and it all comes down to this – this moment in time where we become one.

A united family.

A broad smile instantly crosses my face as the thought runs through my mind.

I inhale deeply. What the fuck is taking them so long? I turn back to Ben who is sitting in the front row. "What time did they get back from the beach?" I frown.

Max smirks. "Relax. She's fine. I checked on her half an hour ago. She's ready to go."

I nod nervously and blow out a breath. Ok, relax. I shake my head and look at the ground as my nerves, once again, steal my rationality.

"Here they come," Adrian whispers and my eyes instantly flick to the top of the stone staircase. I see them. First Abbie, then Bridget.

I feel like I can't breathe.

A smile spreads across my face as my girl comes into focus on Brock's arm, the wind whipping through her hair.

She looks gorgeous... and not because she is wearing a sexier than hell wedding dress – although, that could have a lot to do with it.

It's her smile.

Her strength.

Her courage, and the love that has shone through to me since she has been found.

I always knew she was strong, but I had no idea to what depth.

Her eyes lock on mine as she walks down the stairs like a rock star without one single hesitation.

God, I love this woman.

She is wearing a fitted, white satin dress, and her hair is down and full with a large white flower tucked behind one ear. I have never seen anything more beautiful and I feel myself harden as a wave of emotion hits me like a tsunami. Fuck… not *now*.

I have to stop myself from running up the stairs to greet her, to pull her down to me. *Hurry up!*

I watch intently with my heart in my throat and, after what seems like an eternity, she arrives at the bottom of the staircase before making her way to the alter on our ledge.

"Hello." She smiles softly.

"Hello," I whisper, and before I can stop myself, I have her in my arms and I'm kissing her gently on the lips. I haven't seen her all day and I've missed her so desperately. Tash closes her eyes and kisses me back, then again, and before either of us know what's happening, we are kissing passionately and our friends are all laughing.

We eventually pull apart from each other in realization of what we are doing.

Fucking hell, reign it in, Stanton.

There is a time and a place, and at the alter, on your wedding day, with everyone watching isn't it.

The memory of us making out on the dance floor, that first night at Scott's wedding, comes to the forefront of my mind, and I have to bite my bottom lip to hold back my grin

What is it about us and weddings?

The minister moves forward and smiles warmly. "Can you take each others hands please?"

My eyes flick to the minister, Father Joseph. I flew him in from L.A. yesterday. I had to be positive that the marriage was legal, and the only way I could ensure that was to get him here myself.

Natasha and I face each other and she giggles loudly.

"Holy crap. We are getting married!" she exclaims excitedly as she lifts her flower bouquet in the air. Everyone bursts into laughter and I melt as my eyes hold hers. That is such a Natasha thing to say.

And then I'm transfixed.

I watch my beautiful Natasha declare her love with her sacred wedding vows and I watch as she slides the gold band on my finger. I, in return declare mine vows to her and slide the gold band onto her finger.

She slowly leans forward and tenderly places her hand on my cheek and kisses me, sweeter than anything I have ever experienced, longed for with all of my heart. I feel myself well up and blink to stop myself from crying. The love on the ledge, both between us and from our families, is so strong that I'm sure it could be felt from another galaxy, it's such a tangible force. I pull out of her kiss and glance around to see everyone seems to be feeling the same way, all of them wiping their eyes, overcome with emotion. Even Ben has a tear in his eye. Nothing has ever felt so right and so damn well fucking deserved. This is a fight the whole family has fought.

Fought and won.

The victors.

The victor is love.

I desperately wish I could bottle this perfect moment in time so I could replay it again and again throughout my life.

"I now pronounce you husband and wife."

Through teary eyes Natasha laughs, leans closer, and tenderly cups my face.

"Kiss me, my husband."

Our lips touch and I am lost.

Natasha

The weather has been flawless, just like the night. It's still and just coming on to eight o'clock. Joshua and I have been married for approximately three fabulous hours and I can't wipe the stupid smile from my face. A large, long table sits underneath the tree, covered in white linen tablecloths. Overhead branches are adorned with fairy lights, while candles and beautiful flowers embellish the table. We are drinking the most ridiculously expensive champagne known to man and everyone is laughing and chatting loudly. Large lanterns are lit around the perimeter, and music is being piped out to the entire space. It's magical, to say the least. Never, in my wildest of wild dreams, could I have imagined that I would get married in such a heavenly place. We have just eaten a beautiful meal and now we're all mingling and laughing. This is the most relaxed we have both been for a very long time, and I feel a deep, sated happiness, relieved that we have finally done it.

We are legally married.

I keep catching Joshua looking at the ring on his hand while talking as if not believing it has actually happened. I know how he feels. I can hardly believe it myself.

The waitresses pour everyone another champagne and Joshua stands at the table. Cameron taps the side of his glass with his fork and everyone takes their seat back at their designated spaces. I sit next to Joshua and he places his hand on my shoulder affectionately.

The table falls silent as they wait for his speech, and he seemingly pulls himself together, as if preparing to be serious.

He smiles and swallows nervously. "I would like to thank everyone for coming to celebrate with us." He raises his glass as if finished and everyone laughs. Oh, he's nervous. My heart melts for my beautiful man and I grab his hand in a reassuring gesture.

He hesitates as his face falls solemn and he drops his head. He looks to the empty place next to my mum and the candle that's burning there. My dad's empty place at the table. My eyes instantly cloud over.

"John." He hesitates again and the table falls deathly silent. "There." His voice cracks and he stops. A tear falls onto my cheek and I squeeze his hand just that little bit harder.

"There isn't a day goes by when you are not in my thoughts."

Mum drops her head in sadness but Bridget grabs her hand.

"I go over it again and again. Wondering if I did things differently, would you still be here with us?"

He hesitates and my blurry eyes stare up at him.

Brock drops his head in sadness, too, and I hear Bridget sniff loudly.

"The only relief I have is the hope that you will rest in peace knowing that I will spend the rest of my life ensuring your daughter's happiness. Nobody could ever love her more than I do."

The bittersweet tears run down my face before I quickly wipe them away.

I will not be sad today. I will not be sad today. I will not be sad today.

"More than any other day, I wish you were here today, celebrating our love with us."

Joshua raises his glass. "To John."

Everyone raises their glasses. "To John." They repeat sadly.

He regains his composure and he raises his glass to our guests. "To you lot." He smiles broadly and everyone chuckles. "You have had to endure more in the last few months than any friendship should ever have to endure."

Cameron interjects. "Amen to that!"

Everyone laughs out loud.

Joshua smirks at his beloved brother and continues his speech. "And yet you have all been so loyal and so committed to us." He

17

hesitates and I know he is becoming emotional. "We will never be able to thank you enough for everything you have done and the tears you have shed for us." He raises his glass happily. "To you lot."

Everyone smiles, nods and raises their glass in agreement. "To us lot." They all laugh.

He turns his attention to me, and I smile as I hold my breath.

"Natasha," he whispers.

I smile through my tears.

"For two days I have been trying to get this speech right in my head with what I want to say." He frowns. "But how do I put into words how I feel about you?"

I smile.

"Words fall short," he whispers.

Oh, I love this man. I place my hand over my heart as I literally swoon all over the table.

"There aren't enough words or stars in the sky."

I smile. Could he be any more perfect?

"So I am just going to say it like it is." He smirks.

Abbie and Bridget raise their glasses at me. This speech is going to be super romantic, I just know it. I smile broadly in anticipation.

"You are a beautiful, intelligent, uncoordinated drama queen."

My mouth drops open in horror and the table erupts into laughter. This is not at all what any of us were expecting.

He holds his hands up to order silence as his smile erupts.

"A beautiful slut who I fucking adore."

The table once more erupts into loud laughter. Oh my God, this is the worst wedding speech ever. My eyes flick to Mum who gives me a wink and smiles broadly while I put my hand over my mouth in horror and laugh.

"I can't wait to teach you to ride horses." He raises his brow sarcastically.

My mouth drops open again and I slap his thigh. "Joshua." I laugh.

"And make you wear Jodhpurs." The table's laughter gets louder.

Oh, this is beyond pale.

"Not happening." I smirk, as I shake my head.

He holds his hands up to quieten everyone back down again. "No, no. On a serious note."

Everyone listens attentively and he bends to kiss the back of my hand – a simple gesture that means so, so much to me.

"I love you with all of my heart."

Everyone gushes, and I melt.

He raises his glass for the final time. "To Natasha. My love. My life." He raises his eyebrows cheekily. "My wife." The table cheers loudly. "And her breathtaking smile."

CHAPTER 2

I STAND AT THE handrail and stare out to ocean as the sea breeze whips over my skin. My thoughts are on my father and the fun he would have had here tonight. It's a bittersweet moment of reflection, one that I know every member of our family has felt heavily, today more than ever.

He is deeply missed, but with every dark thought that I have, a new thought of hope takes its place.

We did it. We made it. Joshua Stanton is my husband.

I hold out my hand and stare lovingly at the beautiful rings on my finger. They mean so much more to me than mere diamonds and gold. They're a symbol of love and our ultimate commitment. A symbol of our bravery.

Happiness surrounds me. Our families are dancing and laughing loudly as they talk over the music. Joshua is relaxed for the first time since I have returned, and I feel like a huge weight has been lifted from my shoulders. I feel two large, strong hands slide around my waist from behind before soft lips dust my temple.

"Are you ready for bed, Mrs. Stanton?"

I smile broadly, Mrs. Stanton. *That sounds so good.*

"What time is it?" I ask as Joshua starts to slowly kiss my neck from behind.

"Who cares?" he whispers onto my skin.

"We have guests." I smile as my head tilts by itself to the side to give him greater access.

"This is our wedding. It ends when we say it does, and besides, it's after twelve." He nips me and sends goose bumps down my spine.

I smile and continue to stare into the darkness over the water as Joshua wraps himself around me from behind.

I can feel his arousal encase me and I close my eyes to bask in its glow.

"I'm heading off." Mum smiles.

I turn and smile, take her in my arms and squeeze tightly.

"I love you," I whisper.

"I love you too, darling. This has been one of the happiest days of my life."

"Mine, too." I kiss her softly on the cheek. "Thank you for everything, Mum Your support means so much to both of us."

She pulls out of my embrace and wraps her arms around both Joshua and I. "I just want you kids happy."

"Thank you. We are." Joshua smiles, his eyes lingering lovingly on my face as he puts a protective arm around my shoulders. His attention then flickers around to the guards and he signals to Peter who comes over immediately. "Can you walk Victoria back to her room and watch over her, please?"

"Of course."

Mum shakes her head dismissively. "Joshua, I'm fine."

He raises his eyebrows. "I know, but you will be guarded and safe as well as fine."

Mums eyes fall to mine and she rolls them playfully.

Bridget walks over and puts her arm around Joshua, kissing his shoulder before taking my hand in hers. "I think I was the best bridesmaid today."

I smile, and Joshua shakes his head and smirks.

She holds her hands up in an *I've had too much champagne* gesture. "Tell me? When we were walking down the stairs, who looked the daintiest? It was totally me, wasn't it?"

I laugh out loud. Oh, God, where does she come up with this shit?

"Murph was actually, if you must know," Joshua replies dryly.

"Oh, phooey," she calls loudly. Oh, she is really drunk. Joshua, Mum and me all look at one another and smirk.

Joshua catches Ben's eye and calls him over.

"Didge, do you want to go home?" Joshua asks.

Bridget puts her hands on her hips. "No!" she snaps, annoyed. "I'm going out clubbing. I deserve a night out after all the…" She hesitates and waves her hand over between Joshua and I. "Stuff," she blurts out.

Her eyes find Abbie, who is slow dancing with Nicholas. "We are all going out, aren't we Adrian?" she slurs.

Adrian winces. "I'm tired, Didge, I'm turning in. Nick, Abbs and Cam will go out with you."

My heart drops. Oh no. It really is over with Nick and Adrian, I thought they would work it out.

I smile at Ben who is now standing beside us. "Ben will come with you," I reply.

Bridget's face instantly falls and she goes to say something to him, but then wisely holds her tongue.

He narrows his eyes at her in disdain as if knowing what she was going to say. I frown at their interaction, and my eyes meet Mum's, she shrugs slightly. Hmm, what's going on with these two? Are they still seeing each other? I just assumed they were still together… maybe not.

Joshua's hand slides discretely to my behind and he pulls me slightly into his body where I feel his waiting erection.

My husband wants to consummate his marriage.

"I'm taking my husband home." I smile as I pick up Joshua's hand and kiss the back of it.

His eyes hold mine in the best damn *come fuck me* look I have ever seen, and I feel a rush of adrenaline hit me hard.

He leads me by the hand as we kiss everyone goodnight and then he is dragging me up the stairs in double time. The guards wait wisely at the bottom of the steps to give us some much needed privacy.

We get to the top step and, once out of everyone's view, Joshua picks me up like a bride causing me to squeal in delight. He marches toward our bedroom like a man on a mission.

"What's the rush?" I whisper onto his lips as I sweep my tongue seductively through his lips.

"I need you naked and underneath me." He growls. "Now."

I inhale deeply and realise Bridget is right – it is true – *I can smell his testosterone* and it does smell awesome. He's so fucking hot... and he's so fucking mine.

"How are you going to have me, my husband?" I ask a little too sweetly

He smiles deviously. "Any way I want to."

I giggle into his chest as we enter the suite, and I hold my hand in the air to celebrate being carried over the threshold.

"Is that why you married me? To have my body at your beck and call?"

He bites my neck hard. "Fuck, yeah." He growls and I laugh out loud again. He marches through the bedroom door.

"You won't be laughing in a minute when I shut you up," he whispers darkly, throwing me onto the bed, where I bounce and laugh again. He flicks on the pendant lamps placed on either side of the bed and switches the main lights off. Darkness surrounds us and instantly the mood changes from one of fun to one of sinful pleasure. Dear, God, I have missed him so much. I could never live without this, without him. I lie back and watch him take his suit jacket off in slow motion, then his shirt. I know your wedding night is supposed to be sweet and romantic, but I don't want a bar of that. I want my wedding night to be downright dirty and memorable. As if sensing this, Joshua's sexy eyes hold mine and my heart catches in my throat. He's so beautiful. How did I ever get so lucky?

He kicks off his shoes and socks, then wrestles around with his pants.

I watch him for a moment. "What are you doing there?" I frown.

"Fucking Murph!" he snaps as he looks down at his zipper.

"Huh?"

"The dumb prick sewed me into my pants." He wrestles around again with his pants.

My face lights up. "What?" I giggle. This is priceless.

He shakes his head and I burst out laughing. I hear a rip as he finally tears open Adrian's makeshift sewing. With a shake of his frustrated head, he slowly pushes down his black suit pants, and I am blessed with the sight of the hottest black briefs in the history of the world. I can see every muscle on his chiseled body and the hairs on the back of my neck stand at attention.

"Joshua," I whisper, overwhelmed at what his beautiful body and this night mean to me. I crawl over to him as he stands at the side of the bed. His hand gently strokes my hair as he pulls me towards him.

"I need my wife's lips around my cock," he whispers.

I can hardly breathe through excitement but I nod anyway, knowing I desperately need that, too. Using both hands, I slide his briefs down his legs and lick up the length of his thick shaft. I get an idea and my eyes flicker up to his. I need to erase the memories of those sex tapes I watched in that house and I think I know just how to do it.

"Get your phone," I whisper around his cock.

He frowns in question as he looks down at me.

"I want you to film us."

His eyes darken.

"I want you to watch me suck your dick in my wedding dress."

He rips my hair in his hands as if losing control.

"I want to watch this again and again and I want you to fuck me so damn hard tonight that I might break."

He rips away from me and kisses me aggressively. "There's my beautiful slut," he whispers into my lips. "I've missed my girl." He cups my face in his hands as he looks at me tenderly

Emotion steals my ability to speak. Oh, god. I love him. I love him so much.

"Get the camera," I whisper with renewed excitement.

He raises an eyebrow and then smirks as he pulls away from me. He grabs his video camera from the wardrobe, puts it on the sideboard and turns it on. The red light tells me it's running. I pull him toward me and start to slowly fist him as I scatter kisses all over his hipbones.

Joshua stands silently, holding his breath. He cracks his neck hard and I smile. That damn neck crack gets me. Every. Single. Time. There isn't a more orgasmic thing on Earth than when he does that. Joshua's hands cup the back of my head tenderly. His mouth hangs slack as his dark eyes hold mine. I pull out and slowly lick up his length and around his tip.

"I love you," I whisper.

He clenches his jaw as his arousal amps up to another level. He stands and pulls me up by the hand, kissing me deeply as he holds my jaw where he wants my mouth. Josh's lips drop to my neck and he bites me gently as he drops to his knees and slowly licks his lips as his mouth kisses my sex through my dress.

"Mrs. Stanton," he breathes onto my stomach and I smile like an idiot. Slowly standing, he turns me away from him and slides down the zipper at the back of my dress. Gentle lips dust my skin and my head falls to the side. My dress drops to the floor and I hear him inhale deeply. Since I got back, it feels so new, yet so familiar. I will never get enough of this.

I'm wearing a white G-string and corset and I silently thank the Lord I got that little bit of sun this morning.

"Lay down, my beautiful girl," he commands quietly.

I lie down and he dips to go lower, but I pull him back up to my face.

"No, Josh."

He frowns.

"I need to warm you up, Presh."

I subtly shake my head. "No warming up tonight," I breathe.

"I will hurt you."

"That's exactly what I want."

He hesitates.

"I want you to hurt me like it's the first time. I want to feel the burn of your possession. I want to be taken on my wedding night. I need my husband to *own* me."

Joshua's eyes flash with dangerously high arousal, and he gives me that look that he gives, the one where he goes past his physical limits and I know I am about to fucking cop it.

The tension is palpable and he cracks his neck hard.

"This is why I married you," he whispers darkly.

Feeling very proud of myself, I bite my bottom lip to contain my smile.

"You know what I need more than I do," he whispers before he lays me down on the bed and lifts my hands over my head, holding them in his. He kisses me deeply as he starts to rub his rock hard cock back and forth through my dripping wet flesh.

My head falls back in pleasure. He feels so good. So *hard*.

I try to close my legs to try and get some traction.

"Open." He growls and bites his teeth into my neck. His fingers go to my sex and he pulls my lips apart, positioning his cock. I hold my breath. And he pushes in, my eyes close, waiting as he withdraws slowly and thrusts hard again.

Ah, the burn. I have to try and stop myself from wincing.

My legs try to close by themselves. "Open." He growls harder.

This hurts but holy fuck it feels good.

"Can you feel that, Presh?" he whispers darkly.

I wince as he goes deeper with each stroke.

"I own this beautiful cunt. Mine and only mine," he purrs as he starts to pick up his pace.

His jaw hangs slack and he rises, widening his legs to give himself more power and traction. I can see every muscle on his chest and shoulders, a sheen of perspiration covers his beautiful body. He pushes my legs back to the bed and places his hands on the mattress above my shoulders to hold me still. He slams into me and I cry out in pain.

He groans deeply and his eyes roll back. "I can feel every muscle inside of you. You feel so fucking good, Natasha."

That's it, I can't take it anymore. I lift my legs and wrap them around his back. "Harder," I whisper. "I need it harder."

His hand slides underneath my behind, and he starts to lift me to meet his pumping cock as the bed hits the wall with force.

Dear... Fucking... God. My body starts to shudder as I try to hold it off. I close my eyes to try block out the visual of this muscular beast above me – pumping me with everything that he's got, taking what he needs from my body – but I can't. My body lurches forward as an orgasm the size of a freight train rips though my body, and Joshua growls as he, too, comes in a rush.

We lay panting, gasping for breath and Joshua smiles into my lips as he kisses me tenderly.

"I love you," he whispers.

Emotion fills me. "I love you, too, baby."

Joshua looks to the camera on the side table and winks deviously. "My wife is one hot fuck."

The sun is shining, as I lay on the deck chair, content in a post orgasmic glow. It's about two in the afternoon and Joshua and I have been married for three blissful days. Today is the first day we have had our families around. Up until now we have been alone and have gone from our bed, to the shower, to the pool and not much farther.

We needed some alone time and I have been fucked every which way and eaten every beautiful kind of food on the planet.

This is happiness. Deep sated happiness.

Joshua is still on edge. He watches me wherever I go, scared to take his eyes off of me in case I disappear again.

We have issues to deal with, both of us. I'm pushing them to the back of my mind for the moment. I can't deal with them yet. I'm not sure I even want to. How do you deal with the shit that we have been through? The police interviews were extensive and thankfully I have been cleared of any wrong doing. My main mission at the moment is to make Joshua at ease and get some weight back on him. I think he's lost about ten kilos since I disappeared.

I stand at the kitchen bench and dial Jeston's number; I need to talk to him. Joshua is running on the treadmill and I have some time to myself. The last time we spoke, he was telling me that he thought he loved me and I was being rude. So much has happened since then and I know he put aside his hate for Joshua to try and help find me. I am so grateful and I owe him a huge thank you.

"Tash" He answers on the first ring, he sounds relieved.

Oh, it's good to hear his voice. "Jes." I smile.

"Are you ok?" he breathes.

"I am."

"Fuck, I thought you were dead."

"Thankfully not." I half laugh.

"Tash, it's so good to hear from you."

"Thank you so much for helping everyone try to find me."

"I'm just so glad you are ok."

The line falls silent and I know I have to tell him.

"I got married Jes. Three days ago in Thailand," I whisper as I close my eyes.

He doesn't answer.

"Jes?" I ask. Is he still on the line?

"What do you want me to say?" he breathes.

My heart drops, I do really care for this man. "Congratulations?" I ask hopefully.

"Congratulations," he replies dryly.

"I love him, Jes. He makes me so happy."

He hesitates. "He's a lucky man."

I smile as my eyes tear up. "Can we be friends? Please?"

"Of course."

I feel uncomfortable, I know I shouldn't, but I feel guilty for talking to him when I know he has feelings for me. I should get off the line.

"I will see you next time I come to Australia?" I ask.

"Yeah, sure," he replies sadly, and I know I have hurt his feelings with my dismissal.

I close my eyes and stay silent.

"Bye, Tash. It's good to hear from you."

"Bye, Jes," I whisper through unshed tears.

We both stay on the line, neither one of us wanting to hang up.

I want to tell him I miss him, but I stop myself, this isn't helping either of us. I reluctantly end the call.

That was a lot harder than it should have been and I know in my heart that the girl who finally tames Jesten Miller is going to be a very lucky girl.

It's late in the afternoon and Joshua is swimming in the pool with Didge while I am sitting between Nicholas and Margaret. Everyone else is gathered around the barbeque at the back of the pool area, watching the chef cook an amazing seafood meal, they are laughing and joking. This is a happy time and we are all so grateful that things turned out the way that they did. Just a week ago I was presumed dead and Joshua was in prison for my murder.

"Do you want another drink?" Margaret asks both Nick and I.

"Yes, please," we both reply, and she stands, disappearing to the bar.

My eyes glance to Nicholas as he watches Adrian. I need to hold my tongue. I desperately want to ask him what's going on between them but I will have to wait to get Adrian on his own. I don't have that type of relationship with Nicholas and it would be rude of me to ask him. I know Nicholas still cares deeply, I can tell by the way he watches Adrian. It's sad if they don't work it out. I guess sometimes love really isn't enough. My eyes wander to Bridget and Joshua in the pool. They're laughing as they talk about something, and Bridget is dancing around mimicking something. The bond between them is strong, I can tell they relied heavily on each other when I was gone. I am grateful that they had each other. We're going out tomorrow night and I am looking forward to catching up and relaxing. It's been a too long since I spent time with my friends. Margaret's phone beeps to signal a text and I pick it up off the table in an attempt to give it to her, accidentally reading the message as it flashes up.

It's from Deidre.

I've told her everything.

I frown. *I've told her everything* – what the hell is that supposed to mean? Who is Deidre? That's random, and my eyes rise up to Nicholas as he watches me intently. Shit. Busted spying, I change the subject. "Have you spent any time with Margaret over the last month?" I ask nervously.

He smirks as if he has been expecting this question. "Yes."

I raise my eyebrows in question. "And?"

He bites his bottom lip as his eyes flick back over to his beloved Adrian. "She seems to be doing well."

I fake a smile. "Great," I lie.

Hmm, that's code for... I don't know what? Is something going on with her that I don't know about?

What does I've told her everything mean? Who is 'her' and who is Deidre? What's to tell?

Margaret walks back over to the two of us followed by a man with a tray of two frozen Margaritas and a green drink of some kind. "Thank you." I smile as I take mine.

Joshua gets out of the pool and his eyes meet mine and he smiles softly. I can feel myself melt into his gaze, so I blow him a kiss. He holds his arm out for me and I stand to make my way over to him where he kisses me gently on the forehead and wraps his arms around me.

"You ok?" he whispers.

I nod and smile. "I am now."

"How long till we can go to our room?" He kisses me gently.

I smirk. "Not yet."

The next few hours are a blur of friends, laughter and my stupid self-analysis. I lay with my head on Joshua's lap as we all sit around the fire pit. Who texted Margaret? Why am I so damn suspicious of that text? Is it my gut instinct or am I just so untrusting of people now that I don't know what to think? Robert and Margaret don't seem to talk much; in fact, if I didn't already know they were married, I would never guess they were even together. I wonder if they are still trying to work things out? Margaret is sitting at a table with Scott and his wife, and Robert hasn't been near her for hours. Hmm.

"You ready for bed, Presh?" That husky sexy voice purrs.

I smile. "I am. Are you?"

He nods sleepily and yawns. "Yes."

We say our goodbyes and make our way to our bedroom. I'm tired, but how is it possible to be this tired from doing nothing? I turn the corner to walk into our room and stop dead in my tracks. Joshua runs into the back of me.

"What's wrong?" He frowns.

My eyes stay fixed to the small chocolate, leather bound diary that sits on my bed. I feel my heart start to beat rapidly in my chest.

"Where did that come from?" I stammer as my breathing tightens.

Joshua frowns as he walks past me into the room. "What?"

"The diary."

"Oh, I got Cameron to pick you up a new one today," he replies casually.

Are you kidding me? I pick it up in a rush and carry it into my wardrobe, I throw it into a drawer and slam it shut.

"I don't want a diary!" I snap.

Joshua stands still and frowns as he assesses me for a moment. "Ok. Why not?"

I rip the blankets down with force. "I just don't."

He puts his hands on his hips as he watches me, his eyes drop to the six chunky bangles on my wrist that cover my scar, and I cover them with my hand, suddenly self conscious. "What?" I snap and storm into the bathroom and turn the shower on. God, how dare he buy me a fucking diary? Why would I want to write down the shit that is in my head?

I get into the shower and turn the water on as hot as I can stand it. Joshua, wisely, stays in the bedroom. I lean against the tiles with my heart beating through my chest in anger and I don't even know why. That's a lie, I do but I can't rationalise it. *Just calm down, just calm down,* I keep repeating to myself, and eventually

I do. Forty minutes later, feeling very drained, I exit and slowly dry myself, wrap a towel around my body and walk into the bedroom. Joshua is sitting, propped up against the headboard reading a book. He doesn't look up and I crawl into bed feeling unstable. He leans over and kisses me gently on the lips.

"You ok?" he asks softly, his worried eyes hold mine.

I nod and fake a smile. I have never felt so far from ok. I feel overwhelmed and unstable and unsure why I'm feeling like this. I am home, I am safe. Why is this anxiety still with me? Am I having a panic attack? Is that what this is? Normally I would have a migraine if I get like this but there is no sign. In fact, I would welcome that feeling over this.

"Goodnight, my precious girl. Go to sleep, baby. I'm here, it's ok."

I nod nervously, lie down and turn my back to him. I concentrate on regulating my breathing as he rests his hand on my hip and soothingly rubs his hand in a circle on my behind. I feel myself slowly start to relax under his hand.

It works, and after ten minutes with my love in our bed, I don't remember anything else.

Joshua

I jump off the speeding treadmill, panting. I'm wet with perspiration, so I grab a towel to wipe myself. Nicholas has just returned from his morning run and I need to talk to him. Standing by the gate that leads from his villa into the pool area, I see him stretching.

"Hey." I smile as I approach him.

He nods. "Beautiful morning."

I nod and hesitate. Maybe now is not the time to broach this subject.

"Did you give it to her?" he asks.

I nod.

"Did she write anything down?"

I shake my head. "No." I bought that diary yesterday on Nicholas' suggestion. He's worried about Natasha. I'm worried about Natasha. She's acting normal, as if she has been through nothing, but last night her mask slipped a little and I know she's struggling.

"She was agitated that the diary was there. She threw it into a drawer annoyed."

Nicholas nods. "I see."

I wipe the perspiration that keeps appearing on my forehead.

"Its very early days, Joshua."

I nod. "I know."

"Have you discussed what happened to her at all?"

I shake my head. "I don't want to upset her."

"Has she asked you about your time in prison or anything?"

I shake my head and frown. "No, she hasn't and it's weird. She normally asks me ten thousand questions a day."

"Do you want me to spend some time with her?"

I put my hands on my hips to think. The last thing I want to do is upset her. "Maybe we are worried for nothing and she really is fine?" I shrug.

He smiles. "Perhaps."

"She's a strong woman."

"She is."

We are interrupted as Natasha saunters through the gate in her gym clothes. My eyes drop down to what she is wearing and the thick sweatband around her right wrist.

"Good... morning." I frown. "Why are you up so early?"

"I need to work out," she replies casually.

My eyes flick to Nicholas. What the hell? She hates working out with a passion.

She walks past us and saunters down the path toward the gym, seemingly without a care in the world.

My eyes meet Nicholas' and I shake my head.

"Oh, and Joshua," she calls out.

We both turn to face her. "Can we go motorbike riding today?" she asks. "Yes of course."

"But I want my own bike this time."

I hesitate before I answer.

"Nicholas you are coming, too. It's so much fun." She smiles as excitement fills her face.

"Sure, I would love to," he replies.

Natasha smiles warmly and disappears out of our sight.

I turn my attention back to Nicholas. "We've got a fucking problem."

Natasha

We sit around a large, circular dinner table at a quaint, authentic Thai restaurant, just down from Joshua's house. We've had a fun and action packed day motorbike riding around the Island. Wilson, Scott and Alyssa flew back home to Australia this afternoon, and Margaret and Robert are leaving tomorrow. The parents have met us for one last hurrah.

Joshua has his arm slung over the back of my chair protectively as he talks to Cameron, and I smile as I watch them. I know I gave them a heart attack with my motorbike riding skills today, but I made a resolution to myself when I was escaping and running though the forest, that if I got out of there alive, I was never going to be governed by fear again. I'm going to live life to the fullest and, I'm sorry, but Joshua is going to have to learn to live with it. He stopped the bike a few times and had a tantrum, ordering me off. Even Brock, Max and Bridget were on his side.

I raise my glass at Abbie across the table and she gives me a knowing wink. She seems to be the only one who gets me at the moment. It was me and her owning the road today. Is this how she feels all the time? Like any day could be her last and she needs to have fun at all costs. Is that why she's so brave and doesn't give a fuck about tomorrow?

Today is the most normal I have felt since I returned home and I think its because Joshua was being openly hostile with me. I like my hostile man. I've missed my hostile man. I feel like I want to push all the boundaries and make him control me, and I'm not sure where this is coming from, but I really don't care.

My eyes flick to the door of the restaurant. Where is Mum? She's with Peter and they were supposed to be here half an hour ago. I decide to give her a quick call.

"Can I use your phone?" I ask Joshua.

"I don't have it with me." His thumb gently circles on my collarbone and he smiles sexily. Hmm, hot, edible man.

I smirk and look around the table. Nobody has their phone. We were all riding bikes the whole day. Margaret's phone is on the table in front of her.

"Can I use your phone, Margaret, to call Mum, please?" I ask.

"Sure, love." She swipes in her code and hands it to me as she gets up to go to the bathroom. I dial Mum's number.

"Hello, love. We are around the corner," Mum answers.

"Ok." I smile and hang up.

Everyone is deep in discussion around the table and my eyes flicker around guiltily, dropping to the phone in my hand. Before I can stop myself, I drop the phone down to my lap to shield it from the others and click into call register.

Deirdre

Deirdre

Deirdre

2:00 a.m. this morning. A two-hour call to Deirdre.

Who is fucking Deirdre?

I frown and swipe through to contacts and click on Deirdre's phone number.

0414356232.

Shit, how do I remember this number?

Try to remember the last four digits.

6232, 6232, 6232 I repeat in my head.

I swipe the phone off and pass it back up the table.

6232, 6232, 6232 I repeat.

The table is full of deep conversation, and Max and the other guards are at the table next to us. Who is Deirdre? Why so many calls? How could she have a two-hour conversation with her in the middle of the night and not wake Robert? I don't know, and I don't even know why I am thinking about this shit?

"Are you hungry, Presh?" Joshua gently kisses the side of my face as he tucks a piece of my hair behind my ear.

I smile at my beautiful man. "I am, are you?"

He smiles darkly and his eyes drop to my lips. "Not for food."

I bite my bottom lip to stifle my smile. Truth be known, I think Joshua liked screaming at me today, too. It felt normal that he was angry with me – a relief, even.

"What would you like for dessert, Joshua?" I whisper.

He bends and whispers into my ear. "I think you know, my beautiful slut." His breath on my neck gives me goose bumps and a shudder of excitement runs through me.

I will never tire of this conversation, of this feeling.

Three hours later, dinner is over and, after going for a long walk and stopping at a bar for a drink, we have arrived back in our home.

"I'm having a shower, Presh. Are you coming?" Joshua kisses me on the forehead as he walks past me sitting in the lounge.

"Yes, be there in a minute."

I watch him disappear into our bedroom, and without

thinking, I pick up his phone from the coffee table. As if on auto-pilot, I scroll through his contacts until I get to the one I want.

James Brennan: 0414356232.

I close my eyes in regret.

Holy fuck.

CHAPTER 3

SNOOPING. THE DOUBLE edged sword. The Heaven to my Hell.

You think you want to know something, but then you wish you didn't know it. Margaret has been speaking to James Brennan, not just once, but a lot of times. Two hours in the middle of the night. How do you speak to an abuser that you hate for two hours? What is there to say?

I lay in bed as I go over the conversations Margaret and I have had before in regards to James. She said she loved him at one stage, but then he turned into an abuser and she hated him. Was that just all fucking bullshit? Did he really beat her? Did Robert beat her and she has used James as a cover? What the hell is going on?

I hear Joshua fussing around in the kitchen and the sound of the shaker with ice. I smile. My man is back on his protein. This is a good sign. Normalcy is returning to his life.

He walks in while taking a sip and sits on the end of the bed. "Morning, Presh."

I smile at his I've-been-to-the-gym glow of perspiration. "Good morning, Mr. Stanton."

He smiles sexily at my playful tone. "What would my wife like to do today?"

"Hmm, let me think." I smirk.

He bends and kisses the top of my foot as he runs his hand

up under the blanket towards my thigh. "Do you need a wake up fuck?" he whispers as his eyes drop to my lips.

"Sex maniac," I mouth.

He winks mischievously as he bends and kisses my thigh through the sheet.

"How long are we staying here?" I ask.

"How long do you want to stay?"

"A bit longer." I grab his hand. "I don't want to go back just yet."

"Of course, but I will have to work from here, though, and I do have to be back in two weeks for a meeting."

"Ok." I smile gratefully. "What time do your parents leave?"

"I think their flight leaves about seven tonight."

I nod and I look out of the window towards the ocean in thought.

"We will have lunch with them today, if that's ok? I may not see them for a while. They've both dropped everything for us for six weeks. My father needs to get back to work on Monday."

My eyes meet his. "Are him and your mother working it out?"

He shrugs. "I don't know, I haven't asked. Their fucked up relationship hasn't been on the top of my agenda."

"Hmm." My mind ticks over at a million miles per minute.

"What's happened with James Brennan?" I ask. "Did you ever have him charged?"

He shakes his head. "No, with all the shit that went down, in the grand scheme of things, he was forgotten."

My eyes hold his. "Did he pay you back the money?"

He raises his eyebrows. "Funnily enough, Murph said it hit my account yesterday."

I frown. What the hell is going on? Maybe she was just talking him into paying the money back?

"What's going on with your father and him?"

Joshua gets off the bed and walks into the bathroom. "I don't know and don't care. Dad said he was taking care of it. God knows what that means?"

"Is James still married?" I call out.

"Fuck knows," he calls back.

Hmm, why doesn't he know anything? God, he's annoying. I need to get some answers. I get out of bed, quickly dress and head outside while Joshua showers. Max is sitting out the front garden reading the paper and another guard is at the front, sitting by the main gates, reading a book. Max looks up, sees me and smiles broadly.

"Hello," he says through a smile.

My heart melts a little. Oh, I do love Max. "Hi." I smile in return. "You ok? I feel like we have hardly spoken since I got back."

He nods. "Are you ok is the real question?"

"Yes, I'm good."

His smile turns down sympathetically.

I hesitate before I ask. "Max, are Margaret and Robert staying in the same hotel room?"

He seems taken aback with my question and frowns. "I don't believe so."

Oh, right. I pause to think for a minute. "How long since they have slept in the same room?"

"I'm not sure, not since Joshua went to prison. I stayed at the house to watch over Bridget and your mother and they had separate rooms at that time."

I narrow my eyes. "So, like, six weeks or so?"

He nods and his eyes hold mine. I know he wants to ask what's going through my head but is choosing to be polite instead.

"Do you think they are still together?" I hesitate. "I mean, based on their body language?"

"I wouldn't think so." He shrugs.

I nod. Ok. Interesting. "You ok if we hang here for a while longer? I don't want to go back for another couple of weeks."

"I think I could handle that. Just." He smiles. "This is such a terrible location to work from."

I laugh as I look around. "It is pretty cool here, isn't it?"

He raises his eyebrows at my nonchalance. "You could say that."

I feel him before I see him, and when I turn, Joshua is standing in the doorway. He has obviously been looking for me as he smiles a relieved smile.

"I was just asking Max if it's ok if we stay here for a couple more weeks," I blurt out in a guilty rush.

Joshua's eyes flick to Max.

Max smiles with a curt nod.

"Of course, sweetheart," Joshua replies softly.

I frown at the sympathy sweetheart. My eyes wander between the two men and I notice they seem to know something that I don't.

"You two seem to be getting along very well."

"We are," Joshua replies flatly.

I continue to look between the two of them and I smirk. "It's creepy."

Max laughs out loud while Joshua shakes his head and smacks me on the behind.

"You two are like friendly creepers now. It's weirding me out."

Max shakes his head and rolls his eyes at Joshua who laughs in response.

"I thought you wanted us to be friendly creepers?"

I look at him and raise my eyebrows.

"I'm friendly and Max is the creep."

I smirk and walk back inside. "Bye, Max," I call over my shoulder.

"Goodbye, Natasha."

Joshua cuddles me from behind as I walk. "I need to work today, Presh."

"That's ok," I reply. "I'm on my way to see the girls and Adrian." My face falls. "Is Adrian working today, too?"

"No, he has been working nights."

I smile with relief.

Joshua's face lights up. "And this is good because…?"

"This is good because that means I get to see him today."

He kisses me gently on the lips. "Don't forget lunch with my parents."

"Ok. See you." He disappears into his office, and I shower and dress. I exit through the front door and follow the path around until I get to Adrian's place. Cameron is sitting on the front steps in the sun.

"Mrs. Stanton." He smiles.

I grin as a rush of excitement fills me. I rub my hand through the top of his hair. "You know it, baby. Is Adrian inside?"

"No, I think he's at the girls' place."

"Ok, thanks." I continue walking until I get to their house, and I can hear laughter coming from Mum's bedroom. I smile and go to investigate.

"You can't be serious." Adrian winces as he throws what looks like a shirt out of Mum's wardrobe.

"Deadly." Mum frowns as she picks up the discarded shirt from the floor.

Bridget and Abbie are lying on Mum's bed, curled up in fits of laughter.

"What's going on?" I ask.

Adrian comes out of Mum's wardrobe and places his hands on his hips. "Your mother asked me to give her a makeover, but now that I'm in her wardrobe, she won't let me throw anything out."

I smile and turn my attention to Mum.

"He's trying to throw out my best clothes." She shakes her head in disgust.

Adrian pinches the bridge of his nose. "God, give me strength," he whispers to himself, and I a giggle. Mum is the worst person to style, she has things in her wardrobe she has had for twenty years. This styling project is long overdue. He disappears back into the wardrobe and I flop onto the bed in between my two friends to watch the show.

"This is going." He throws a handbag out onto the floor.

"No, it is not. That is a beautiful piece."

"Exactly, piece being the key word. It belongs in a museum," Adrian huffs.

The girls and I smile as we listen on.

"I'm glad you think this is funny, bitches." Mum calls from inside the wardrobe.

"Who wants a coffee?" Abbie asks as she rises and disappears to the kitchen.

Bridget takes my hand in hers and we lay together watching Adrian and Mum squabble over what clothes he is throwing out and I smile. How has this beautiful man become so dear to us? He is like a son to my mum... although it's a very different relationship to hers and Brock's. Never in a million years – when I first met Adrian and I thought he was Donatella Versace – did I think I would be laying on a bed watching him clean out my mother's wardrobe.

"Coffee is up," Abbie calls from the kitchen. We all take our seat on the kitchen bench. She has cut up warm banana bread and slathered it in butter.

"I think Joshua and I are going to stay for another two weeks," I mutter as I bite into my bread.

"I'm going to leave in a few days, dear," Mum tells me. "I haven't been to Australia for weeks and Nicholas is leaving on Wednesday when the plane arrives back. That's ok, isn't it? I will come back to L.A. in six weeks or so."

Adrian's face falls. "Is that what Nick said? He's leaving Wednesday?"

"Yes," Mum replies as she, too, bites into her banana bread. "How do you not know this? You are staying with him."

"What's going on with you two?" I frown into my coffee.

Adrian gets up and closes the heavy glass door so that nobody else can hear us. He shrugs sadly. "Nothing." He sighs as he flops back onto his stool.

"God, you're an idiot. Go out there, get butt naked and seduce him in the pool, for fuck's sake!" Abbie snaps.

Bridget and Mum nod carelessly as they shovel their cake into their mouths.

"Maybe not in the pool. I want to swim in that pool," Bridget mumbles with her mouth full. I nod as I pull a disgusted face, and Adrian blows out a deep breath deep in thought.

Margaret knocks on the door. "Ready?" She smiles at mum.

"Give me a second." Mum rushes to her bedroom to get her handbag. They are going shopping.

The girls both stand and go to the door to talk to her as she waits for Mum.

I fake a smile and turn back to my coffee. I don't know what to even think of her, of this. It's another fucking nightmare that I don't need. When she told me back then, when I found her in that hotel, that she was abused by James, I believed her. I would never *not* believe someone who told me they had been raped… but it never did sit right. I always had this gut feeling that something was off with her story, but I guess I put it down to shock. That was the absolute last thing I thought she was going to tell me, and it shocked the hell out of both me and out of Adrian. She was genuinely scared of him in the hotel the night, and yet, here we are, just two months later and she is calling him in the middle of the night. Maybe she was just trying to talk him into paying Joshua the money back. But the text from him said: *I've told her everything*.

The only connection I can make to that comment is that he

has told his wife everything. But why would he tell his wife every-thing when he was black mailing Margaret for so many years with the sole purpose of keeping her quiet?

I was going to say something, but now that I know that her and Robert are not together, I'm not so sure that I should. Is it even rel-evant to anything anymore? The boys know who their biological father is. Robert is no longer being deceived. Am I just going to drag up another ugly can of worms? Nobody knows I know. Ha, that's the thing. I don't even know what I know. I'm just jumping to conclusions here. It's probably completely innocent.

Suddenly, a vision of Amelie lying wet and dead on the ground in the pouring rain comes to me, and I can feel the weight of the heavy gun in my hands.

My face drops as the horrific memory poisons me.

"What is it?" Adrian asks, putting his hand on my thigh in a reassuring gesture.

I jump as I am pulled from my thoughts and shake my head. "I'm sorry. Miles away." I fake a smile.

Adrian's knowing eyes hold mine. "Are you ok, baby?"

My heart rate has risen through the roof and I suddenly feel sickly hot. The sting of perspiration burns my underarms. My eyes tear up and I nod. Please stop, I need these feelings to stop. As if reading my mind, he leans over and grabs my head, pulling it to his. "It's going to be ok," he whispers.

I nod as our foreheads rest together. "I know." Fuck, I hate feeling like this. I hate seeing this shit in my head.

"Do you want me to get Josh?" he asks.

I shake my head as the lump in my throat forms. "N-no," I stammer. "I don't want to talk about it," I croak as I pull myself together

He smiles sympathetically and holds my hand in his, resting it on his lap as his worried eyes linger on my face.

I shake off my dark thoughts. "Are you going to get me some more banana bread or what?"

He smiles in my deployment tactics. "Do you want butter?"

"Totally."

Joshua

I sit in my office and send my fifteenth email of the morning. After not thinking about work for so long, it's now time for me to step up. We are going through some serious damage control and I'm scrambling to please the board. My mind keeps wandering to my father and the conversation I had with him yesterday about James Brennan. Dad aborted the hit while I was in prison, not wanting to put anyone through any more pain. A cop out if you ask me. He also bought James' share of the company from him. They have severed ties completely and he has left it up to my mother if she wants to have him charged by the police or not. Regret fills me. I know this means for certain that he has given up on their relationship, that he just wants to be done with it and walk away.

A knock on the door brings me back from my thoughts. It's Brock.

"Hey," he calls out. "You wanted to see me."

"Hi. Take a seat." I gesture to the chair at my desk and he frowns as he sits. "What's up?"

I inhale deeply. This conversation is going to go one of two ways. He will either lose his shit or he will be with me one hundred percent.

I hesitate.

"Spit it out," he sighs, annoyed at my procrastination.

"Are you still enjoying the special forces?" I lean back and swivel my chair as I hold my pen in my hand.

He shrugs. "Its what I do."

"And the constant deployments?"

"They get to you after a while. It fucks up my personal life pretty bad." He shrugs again. "But I'm used to it."

"I have a business proposal."

He shakes his head and holds up his hands. "No, thanks. I am not working for you."

I run my tongue over my top teeth. Brock still has the ability to piss me off easily. No doubt he always will.

"I don't want you to work for me," I respond.

His eyes hold mine.

"How would you like to own your own private investigation company?"

He looks at me, his face serious. "I'm listening."

"One that worked for people like me to..." I hesitate, how do I word this? "... seek out the scum."

I stand and walk over to the window.

Brock screws up his face. "Oh, fuck off. You have been watching too much damn television. Private investigation company? What is this, CSI? Give me a break."

I turn to face him. "These businesses are flourishing, Brock. It's where I got Ben in the first place. An agency just like this."

He folds his arms in front of him and, despite his protests, I know I have piqued his interest.

"So, it works like this: you have security personal working for you. Ex special forces... Ex-police, Marines, Army, Navy – Men and women who know what they are doing. Clients can hire bodyguards from you or you can take personal jobs on for a fee. I will fully bankroll the business and it will be yours to do with as you please."

He sits back in his chair. "Not interested," he replies flatly.

"You will hear me out, at least," I snap.

He rolls his eyes and blows out a deep breath. "Whatever. Go on."

"I *will* bankroll it."

"How much is bankroll?"

"All expenses, plus your current salary... quadrupled."

"Oh, please. You would really do all of this to keep your wife's brother in the states? This is ludicrous."

I lift my chin in annoyance. Are we going to fight about this? "It's not in the states. I want it run out of Australia."

He narrows his eyes. "Why Australia?"

"I have your first job all lined up. I will be your first client."

He sits back in his chair. "What is it?"

"Track and find Coby Allender's accomplice and hand him into the police."

He stares at me.

"Natasha is not setting one foot on Australian soil with those sick fucks interested in her, and I know it's only going to be a matter of time before she wants to go home to see her mother."

"How would I find him?"

I shrug. "You're the special forces, you tell me. If you can't, hire someone who can."

He shakes his head.

"They are murdering innocent women for fun. I can't live with myself knowing I could have done something to stop it or helped in some way."

"Why don't you find them yourself?" He sneers.

I screw up my face. "I'm not taking Natasha to Australia to be the bait, and I know computers, not how to track criminals. I know nothing about this twisted shit."

He narrows his eyes, obviously deep in thought.

I hold up my hands. "Don't give me an answer now. Think about if for a few days. I have spoken to Ben and he is prepared to help you get started. He knows what he is doing, this is his field."

"Will Ben work for me?" he asks, for the first time I see a genuine spark of interest from him.

"Not if I can help it," I reply honestly. "I want Ben with me."

"I think Ben wants out of here."

My eyes hold his. The thought had crossed my mind. He mentioned going back to South Africa yesterday. "He is just adjusting to things. He will get over it."

He raises his eyebrows in a we-will-see gesture.

"How many staff would I hire?"

I shrug. "Probably start with five men. I have contacts and can get you bodyguard gigs straight away, but I'm sure once word gets out, private jobs will start rolling in."

"And it would be completely my business?"

I nod. "I want nothing to do with it. Adrian will deal with the finance and that is as far as I want to know. You can sell it down the track if you want and go back to your present job. I don't give a shit. I want Allender found now. That is my priority."

He raises a brow and stands to shake my hand. "I will have a think and let you know."

Natasha

"Table for four," Joshua asks the waiter at the restaurant.

The kind looking man gestures to a table in the corner. "This way, please."

Joshua puts his hand in mine and we walk to our seats in the cosy corner. We are meeting his parents for lunch, and quite frankly, I would rather have a tooth pulled out.

"Would you like any drinks?" The waiter asks as he pulls out my chair.

Joshua gestures to me and I narrow my eyes as I think. "Can I have a bottle of Sav Blanc, please?"

Joshua raises a brow. "Ok then," he mutters under his breath. The waiter turns his attention to Joshua.

"I will have an iced water with lemon."

Hmm. I look at him, my face deadpan. Why is he so damn healthy all the time?

I see Robert first, and then Margaret. They smile as they enter and Margaret falls into the seat in front of me, placing her wallet and phone on the table. "Hello." She smiles.

"Hi," I force out.

Joshua smiles and turns his attention to ordering some drinks for his parents. I turn my attention onto Mrs. Shifty sitting opposite me. *What the fuck are you up to, bitch?*

"Have you had a good day?" she asks.

"I have. How was shopping?"

"Oh, I didn't really find anything. It was more your mother who wanted to go."

I fake a smile. Is she insinuating that my mother needs to shop because she has nothing? *Stop it. You are being a drama queen. That's not what she meant and you know it.*

"What time is your flight?" Joshua asks Robert.

"We have to be at the airport at 5.30 p.m."

"We have had a wonderful time, darling," Margaret gushes as she grabs Joshua's hand over the table.

I watch her intently. Fuck, she is pissing me off just by breathing.

"We are so happy that things turned out the way they did." Robert smiles and I smile my first, genuine smile since they arrived.

"How long are you kids staying?" Margaret asks.

"About another ten days or so," Joshua replies as he puts his hand on my leg.

"Are you going back to your house in L.A.?" he asks.

"Umm, not sure yet." Joshua's eyes flicker to mine. "We haven't really decided where we want to live yet, have we?"

"No, not yet." My anxiety rises. I don't know where I want to live, but I definitely know it's not in Joshua's beloved house. I have watched it through those evil cameras of Amelie's too many times and it freaks me the hell out.

Margaret's phone dances silently across the table and the name Deidre comes up on the screen. My fury ignites.

She holds up a pointer finger to signify she will just be a minute. "Hello, Deidre," she answers.

I start to hear my angry heart beat in my ears.

Go time.

She holds her hand over the phone and whispers. "I won't be a minute. I will just go outside to take this call."

"Of course," Joshua replies, preoccupied with his father.

She stands, walks to the front of the restaurant, then out of the front door.

What do I do? What do I do? My legs bounce as I think. What the hell is she saying to him?

That's it.

"I'm going to the bathroom," I mouth to Joshua, and he nods as he talks.

I walk over to the bathroom and Max frowns at me as he follows me. My eyes dart around to Joshua to check I'm not discovered before I take off out of the front door.

"What are you doing?" Max growls quietly at me.

"I'm just seeing Margaret. I won't be a minute. Wait inside, please."

"No." He follows me out.

I look around frantically, spotting Margaret standing behind a pillar around the corner of the driveway. I walk over next to her to listen without being seen.

I do a shoo symbol with my hand at Max. He narrows his eyes and stands to the side.

"Yes, darling, I know," she says gently.

She listens.

"I will be home tonight."

She listens.

"Tomorrow."

I frown. What the hell? She is meeting him *tomorrow*?

"I will ring you in the morning for the address."

She listens.

"I can't wait to see you, too."

What?

"Terribly," she replies.

Oh my God, he just asked her if she missed him. What the hell?

"I love you, too."

My mouth drops open in shock. I don't fucking believe it.

She walks around the corner and runs straight into me. Her face falls. "Natasha, darling. What are you doing out here?"

I glare at her.

"I was just talking to my friend, Deidre," she mutters nervously.

I continue to glare at her. I'm too angry to even speak. I fold my arms in front of me and narrow my eyes.

"You can cut the shit now, Margaret."

Her face drops. "What do you mean?"

"That was James on the phone. I'm not an idiot."

She raises her eyebrows. "James? Don't be ridiculous."

"Shall we take your phone out and compare it to James' number on Robert's phone."

Her face drops. "Why are you spying on me?" she snaps angrily.

"So, you did lie? The whole fucking thing was a lie?" I fume.

She shakes her head. "No. No. It was all true."

"He blackmailed you."

She stares at me hopelessly as she tries to think of an answer.

"He never even beat you did he?"

She doesn't answer.

"*Did he?*" I yell.

"Natasha, please. It's complicated. You wouldn't understand."

53

"You're right. I wouldn't." I sneer. "You're pathetic."

"He doesn't mean to hit me."

I scrunch up my face in confusion. "So, he *does* hit you?"

"He just loses his temper."

"Why?"

Fake tears well up in her eyes. "Because I won't leave Robert for him."

"What the hell?" I cry. "What are you fucking saying?"

"We have been…" she hesitates as if thinking of her wording, "involved for a long time. I could never leave Robert because I was scared Joshua would find out."

"So, the rape story was a lie?" I yell. I can't believe this bitch. Who makes up stories like that?

She shakes her head. "No, he has raped me in the past and he does hit me. But only because he loves me."

"He hits you and rapes you because he loves you? Have you gone completely mad? Are you listening to what you are saying at all?"

"He so desperately loves me. So much so that he can't stand the thought of me going home to Robert. He has even threatened to kill me, to kill himself if I don't see him."

I don't believe this. She is defending his behaviour. She's in a domestic violent relationship with him.

"I love him, Natasha." Her eyes search mine.

I stand still on the spot as everything I thought I knew falls into place.

This was my gut feeling.

I shake my head in disgust.

"You are a lying, two faced bitch."

Her face falls. "Natasha, please understand."

"No!" I shout back. "I understood when you told me the lies. I understood when you kept Joshua and I apart, knowing all along that we were not cousins."

"Natasha, please. My marriage to Robert is over. It doesn't need to be bought up."

I fake a smile. "Fuck you. My understanding is over. Get out of my life."

I pace back and forth along the side of the pool at mine and Joshua's house. I'm panicking. I don't know if I am doing the right thing or not, but I am not covering for that bitch one minute longer. I've just sent Joshua and Cameron a text telling them that I need to see them both immediately. They were relaxing by the pool at Cameron's house.

Sorry to be the party pooper, boys.

They come through the gate together, and I know instantly that Joshua knows something is wrong, I can read it on his face.

"What's up?" Cameron asks.

I fake a smile and gesture to the seats by the pool, watching them as they both sit down.

I continue to pace back and forth as I try to regulate my heartbeat.

"What's wrong, Natasha?" Joshua asks.

I turn to face them and swallow the bucket of sand in my throat.

"So…" I pause. God, I'm going to sound like a stalker. A creepy troublemaking stalker.

"So what?" Joshua asks with agitation, obviously annoyed at my procrastination.

"You know the other day when I was sitting by the pool with your mum and Nicholas?"

They both frown and shake their head. "No, but go on," answers Cam.

"Your mum's phone was on the table next to me."

They both sit still.

"Anyway." I keep pacing. I already hate this conversation. "She got a text and I went to hand it to her, but I saw it was from someone called Deidre."

Joshua frowns.

"It said: I have told her everything."

"Who's Deidre?" Cameron frowns and Joshua shrugs.

Of course they don't know who Deidre is because she doesn't fucking exist.

I keep pacing as I try to get my wording right in my head. "Well, it played on my mind. I kept thinking, who has she told everything to? That statement... It just doesn't make sense, you know?"

Joshua lays back on the chair as he listens patiently.

"And then, remember, we went to the restaurant, and I wanted to ring Mum, so I borrowed your mother's phone."

Cameron frowns.

This is the awkward stalker part of the story. "I was kind of worried about your mum."

"Why?" Joshua frowns.

I shrug. "I don't know. I can't even put my finger on it. I just was."

He stares at me.

"This is going to sound evil, but I went through her call register and she had been speaking to Deidre at all times of the night for hours."

Joshua sits up. "Who is this Deidre?"

I blow out a breath. "Promise me you won't be mad at me?"

"Why?" Joshua says flatly.

"I memorised the Deirdre's phone number, and when we got home I checked it against the numbers in your phone."

"And?"

"Deirdre is James Brennan."

"What?" Joshua barks.

"And the phone call she got at lunch today was from Deirdre, so I followed her outside to eavesdrop, and I heard her tell him she loved him," I blurt out in a rush.

"Are you fucking kidding me?" Cameron spits.

I shake my head nervously. "She saw me."

"What did she say?" Joshua questions angrily.

My face falls. "She asked me not to tell you."

"Why didn't you tell me this before she got on the fucking plane this afternoon?" Joshua yells.

"I don't know. I didn't want any more drama. Haven't we had enough drama, Joshua?"

He starts to pace.

"And Max told me that your mother and father are not sleeping together in the same room, so I thought maybe they are over and... and I didn't know if I should say anything," I stammer.

"Fucking unbelievable." Cameron sighs sadly.

"I'm sorry," I whisper. "I don't know if I did the right thing, but I am never keeping another secret from you two again. I had to tell you."

Joshua blows out a defeated breath. "So, everything was a lie?"

I shrug. "I don't know."

Joshua rubs his hands through his hair. "I need a fucking drink."

CHAPTER 4

"AND THEN SHE told him she loved him."

"Fuck off." Abbie spits, her eyes wide. I take a sip of my Margarita and nod. "She actually said that?"

"Yep."

"Stupid bitch." Bridget shakes her head. "What did you say?"

"I totally lost my shit and called her a lying bitch or something." I blow out a breath. "I don't even know. I was so mad at her that I can't remember."

"Fucking hell."

"I know," I murmur into my glass.

"I said something lame about her being a lying bitch. I wish I was more prepared. I would have nailed her."

"I hate it when you do that," Bridget says.

"Do what?" Abbie asks.

"You know, like have a fight and think of all the things you should have said long after the fight is over."

Abbie lights a cigar and throws the packet to Cameron who is sitting down the other end of the bench table. He nods in thanks, takes one out and lights it before he passes the packet to Joshua. The dance music is loud and the crowd is noisy. We are at a bar on the beach of Phuket. Its about nine o'clock and we arrived an hour ago. A night out that we all desperately needed. Brock, Ben, Max and the bodyguards are on the table behind us, talking war and horror stories. Joshua and Cameron are sitting on the other end of the table, no doubt discussing the same as we are: The Margaret saga. They took it better than I expected. Joshua said he could tell by my body language when I got back from speaking with his mother at lunch that something had gone on. The sick truth is, I think this is the story we had all imagined, anyway. It's not shocking… more disappointing. I wanted her to be the victim, the misunderstood mother-in-law, and I wanted to be her saviour.

I believed her and defended her, yet, in the end, it had all been a lie. I do believe she is an abused woman, neglected by her husband so seeking love from another man. Unfortunately, that's a man whose only power is to take hers. He's a wimp who blames his obsession and his inability to have her as the reason he abuses her. I know it's common in domestically violent relationships, but when it's someone you know, it's hard to truly understand. He has brain washed her into thinking she brought this on all by herself, and that if she would just do as he asked, he wouldn't need to hit, to rape, and to destroy her self esteem. She has obviously made an allegiance with the pain and needs the violence to feel his love, as if it validated it in some way. Sick, soul destroying and fucked up.

He doesn't deserve her. Who am I kidding? How can you help someone who doesn't want to be helped? They are as messed up as each other.

I am brought back to the here and now by a tall, well-built, blonde man standing next to Bridget. "Would you like to dance?" he asks her in what sounds like a German accent.

Her eyes flick to Abbie's and mine.

"Yes, she would," Abbie splutters.

Joshua and Cameron make eye contact, and Cameron smirks into his drink.

Bridget smiles nervously and he takes her hand, leading her to the dance floor. I look over to Ben for his reaction. He is still sitting at the other table, and his eyes flicker up to her, then he gulps down a large swig of his beer without even tasting it.

"What is she doing?" I whisper to Abbie. "What's going on with her and Ben?" I frown.

"Ben is an asshole." Abbie tuts as her eyes follow Bridget and Blondie through the crowd.

"Why?" I whisper, I'm confused.

"I hope she screws this guy into next week."

"What happened between them?"

We are interrupted by Adrian and Nicholas, as they take a seat at our table. Adrian smiles broadly and kisses both of us on the cheek. "Hello, my beautiful girls."

Nicholas is going home tomorrow and they went out to dinner on their own. I grab his hand under the table and give it a squeeze. Cameron gestures something to Nicholas and he stands and goes over to talk to the two of them. Cameron offers him a cigar, which he accepts.

"Where's Didge?" Adrian asks.

"Dancing with a hot guy."

Adrian sits up on his stool and cranes his neck to see before he lets out a low whistle when he catches sight of him. "Nice," he whispers.

I hold my hands up. "Excuse me. Am I the only one who is batting for Ben here?"

Adrian shakes his head. "That ship sailed and he missed it."

"Here, here," Abbie mutters as she clinks her glass with Adrian's.

I frown and am interrupted by two warm hands slipping around my waist from behind. "Would you like a drink, Presh?" my gorgeous Lamborghini asks.

I lean back into him and he kisses me tenderly over my shoulder. "Yes." I smile against his lips.

"Margaritas?" He looks around at everyone.

"Yes, please." Abbie smiles.

I stand. "I'll come to the bar with you."

He turns and walks through the club and I follow him like

a puppy, my eyes drop to his behind as he walks through the crowded club. He's in a black singlet and coloured board shorts. His ass looks taught, tight and totally fuckable.

I'm feeling more myself tonight. Maybe I just needed to fight with Margaret all along. It felt so good calling her a bitch to her face.

I am wearing a black loose fitted wrap around dress with a black bikini underneath in case we go swimming at the beach on the way home. We get to the crowded bar surrounded with people and Joshua stands protectively behind me, gently sweeping my hair to one side of my neck. The music has a deep beating base, and Joshua slowly kisses my neck.

"If I kiss you here." He kisses me on the neck. "What happens?"

"I would tell you to keep going." I smile against his cheek.

"If I bite you here." He nips me on the neck and I yelp, there it is, my pleasure with my pain. "What happens?"

My eyes close. "I get wet," I whisper, releasing a smile. I like this game.

"Mmm," he murmurs in my ear.

A spot becomes available and we go to the front. He leans over. "I will have two *Cointreau's* immediately, and…" He does an internal count. "Ten Margaritas and ten lagers, please."

The waitress makes the two *Cointreau's* and passes them to us. He pays and gestures to a table over to the side of the bar that is surrounded with people facing the dance floor. "We will be over here."

"Ok, thank you. Ten minutes."

Joshua takes the two drinks and walks through the crowd over to the table and sits down. I follow but before I can speak, he has pulled me onto his lap.

His tongue dives deeply into my mouth. "Joshua, what are we doing over here?"

"I need to feel it."

"Feel what?"

"How wet you are."

My eyes widen. "Here?" I whisper.

He bites my ear from behind.

"But, Ben..." My eyes flutter around to Ben, who is now standing against the wall to keep an eye on us as we go to the bar.

"He can only see our heads, we are shielded by the people and the crowd."

"Joshua."

"He's preoccupied with Bridget." He sighs in frustration.

My eyes flick around and, sure enough, on the other side of the dance floor Bridget is dancing with her German and Ben is watching her like a raging hawk.

And then I feel Joshua's hand slide up the inside of my thigh, underneath my dress, and we're shielded only by the table as I sit on his lap.

"Open your legs."

My eyes widen. "Josh."

His strong fingers push my bikini pants to the side and swipe through my wet flesh,

"Dripping," he whispers into my ear as he starts to kiss my neck. "Nice and creamy." My breath catches. "Just how I need it."

He slowly pushes into me with his two thick fingers and it's all I can do not to close my eyes in pleasure.

"Act normal." His tongue roams up and down my neck.

Fuck, act normal? How in the hell do I do that?

"Wider."

"Huh?"

"Open your legs wider," he orders.

"We are in a club," I whisper at him over my shoulder. I can feel his large erection through his shorts beneath me.

"We are in the dark and you are on my lap under the table, nobody can see."

He pumps me with his fingers gently. From the outside we look like I am just sitting on his lap with my legs wide. But underneath my dress, Joshua's magic fingers are slowly sinking in and out of me. I'm wet, so wet and I am starting to throb. He pushes me hard again and I fall forward onto the table.

"Stop moving," he whispers. "Behave."

I shudder. God, I love this man.

For five minutes, we sit alone in the dark, his fingers working me, my body riding his. We are both quivering as we hold off our arousal. The song *Yeah* by Usher comes on, and I know I have to have him to it.

"Fuck me," I whisper over my shoulder.

His lips take mine aggressively.

"Here?" he pants darkly.

I am trying my hardest to slow my heartbeat. "I need your cock inside of me now."

"Beautiful slut." He growls as he takes my lips again in his hard.

"Lean forward and pick up your drink slowly," he instructs softly into my ear sending goose bumps scattering across my skin.

"What?" I frown.

"Get off my dick so I can get it out."

I bubble up a giggle and slowly lean forward in the dark to lift my drink, I can feel him fiddling with the Velcro on his shorts beneath me and I look uninterested as my eyes flicker around to see if the others have noticed. Surprisingly, nobody has. With one hand, Joshua opens my lips underneath my dress, and the other hand, he places on my hip, pulling me down in one strong motion.

My eyes close.

We stay still, normal and uninteresting to the outside world, but feeling absolute perfection on the inside.

"Natasha." His breath stutters. "You feel so fucking good around my cock, baby."

Usher's sexy voice calls out as a cloud of arousal hangs heavily over me. I can't see, I can't think. I can only feel the large thick muscle that is deep inside my body, throbbing, begging to be fucked hard.

"This cock is yours. Work for it," he whispers.

My eyes close. Oh, dear god.

"Milk me."

I squeeze him hard and we both groan silently.

"I can't move. You need to milk me." He bites my ear.

I clench.

"Harder," he groans softly into my ear.

Oh, fucking hell. My head drops down and I start to slowly clench in a rhythm. His breathing picks up and his hand starts to grip my hipbone with force. He's close, I can feel him swelling inside of me.

We keep going and going and, God, I would give anything for him to throw me across the table and fuck me hard.

My body starts to shudder and I squeeze hard.

One, two, three clenches, and I double over onto the table as he comes in a rush. We stay still, both panting, both lost to our arousal, totally lost to each other.

I sit back and lean my head against his chest as I try to control my breathing, perspiration kissing my skin.

He kisses the side of my face gently and wraps his arms around me and holds me close.

"I should come to the bar with you more often." I smile into his chin.

He smiles deviously. "Don't you mean come at the bar more often."

I giggle loudly and he quickly pulls out and rearranges us both. He picks me up and stands. I turn and face him and his open lips linger on mine.

He looks up as his eyes glance around.

"What are you looking for?"

"A bathroom. My wife needs a clean up."

Joshua sits at the other end of our table, his dark eyes fixed on me. After our foreplay at the bar two hours ago, my man is ready to fuck and fuck hard. He signals to the door discretely with his chin.

I nod. "Ten minutes," I mouth.

My eyes wander around again, finding Adrian. "What do you reckon they are talking about?" I whisper to him.

He raises his eyebrows. "Honestly?"

"Yep." I drain my glass.

"I reckon Brock is telling her how many ways he is going to fuck her tonight."

My lip curls up in disgust. "I was thinking that, too."

We both sit and watch Abbie and Brock deep in conversation as they sit on the next table. My best friend and my brother. God, it's like a bad romance novel on crack.

I shake my head. "Don't get me wrong, I love Abbie. But my brother? Seriously?"

Adrian sips his drink and shrugs. "Well, it's not like either of them is going to get hurt. That's got to be a plus."

I frown. "I don't want Brock getting attached."

Adrian smiles brightly. "I hate to break it to you, but your brother is one of the most sexually dominant men I know. He's not the one getting hurt."

I screw up my face in disgust. "Do you think?"

He raises his eyebrows. "I know it. I've seen him in action."

My face falls. "When?"

"A few times we have been out and here over the last week. Him and Cameron have been carving up."

My eyes roam over to Cameron in the corner. He's with two

gorgeous Spanish girls. My guess is he wants both of them but will take one if its not offered. I'm surrounded by sex maniac players.

I drag my hand down my face in disgust. My eyes flick to Ben who is now openly furious at Bridget.

"What do you reckon is going to happen here?"

Adrian watches Didge dirty dancing on the dance floor. "She's going to sleep with that guy."

"No." I frown. "Really?"

He shrugs. "She's not wired like us two. Why the hell not?"

I nod. "Yeah, I suppose."

Bridget comes stumbling through the club with her German on her arm. She's tipsy and smiling like an idiot. My eyes assess her companion. He is ridiculously masculine.

"Hello." He smiles.

I fake a smile in return and widen my eyes at Adrian.

Adrian mouths the words, "Oh my fucking god." He licks his finger to signify smoking hot.

She bends over to retrieve her bag from the other side of the table and his hand slides down and cups her behind. He squeezes it, whispers something in her ear and she laughs.

His hands come around her from behind and drop to her hip-bones and then lower.

"Get your fucking hands off her." Ben growls.

Our eyes all snap to Ben. Shit. He stands next to us like the incredible hulk. Steam is practically shooting from his ears and his jaw is ticking in anger.

We look back to Bridget in horror. Oh no.

"Guard Natasha Ben and keep your eyes off me." She sneers sarcastically.

She turns and leans up on her toes. "Lets go home, baby," she says to her German.

My face drops in horror.

He smiles deviously and grabs her behind again.

Adrian's and my horrified eyes meet, oh my fucking god. I look around in a panic and see Brock and Joshua both stand at the possible impending fight.

Ben walks right up to this guy's face. "If you want to live… Get the fuck out of here now."

"Make me." The guy sneers.

Oh. My. God. Ben is not someone you mess with.

Ben grabs the German by his throat and holds him at least fifteen centimetres off the ground. Adrian stands in a rush and pulls me by the arm out of the way. Joshua grabs me from him and takes me to the wall and hands me to Max.

"Take Natasha outside."

I shake my head in a panic as I see Ben go ballistic and punch this guy in the face. What the fuck is going on?

The table tips over and all the drinks smash on the floor.

"*Ben!*" I hear Bridget scream. Joshua grabs Bridget and she starts to wrestle with him.

The German punches Ben, but he responds, returning with three quick, hard punches.

Joshua wrestles with Bridget as Brock stands and watches, but doesn't move to break it up.

Max grabs my arm. "Outside, Tash."

"*Break it up!*" I yell.

Max looks at me with a this-guy-deserved-it look.

Max pushes me forward and I stumble out through the front doors. We wait around the side of the building as bouncers run in from everywhere.

"What the hell is going on?" I yell at Max.

Next thing I know, Bridget is being dragged out of the doors by Ben and pulled around to the side of the building.

They don't see us.

"What the fuck do you think you are doing?" Bridget screams.

"What the fuck are *you* doing?" Ben yells in her face.

I shrivel. Shit, Ben is scary when he's mad.

"I'm getting over you," her voice cracks in pain.

Oh, pity fills me. My poor sister is hurt.

Bens face falls. "Bridget," he says softly.

Her face screws up as tears fill her eyes. "Don't!" she cries.

"I-I don't want it to be like this between us," he stammers.

She pushes him hard in the chest. "You did this. Not me."

He runs both of his hands through his hair in frustration. "Bridget," he repeats.

"Why, Ben? Why?"

His haunted eyes hold hers, their hurt evident.

"Answer me!" she screams.

"Come on, Natasha." Max grabs my arm to stop me listening. They don't even realise we are here. I snatch it away. "Shh." I growl.

Ben shakes his head. "I can't be..." He stops as if not knowing what to say.

"What?" she yells.

He doesn't answer.

"You can't be loved, is that it?" she cries.

"Bridget," he says sadly.

"No. Don't you dare Bridget me. You spent every night in my arms, and then when I needed you the most–"

He cuts her off. "It was my fault she went missing."

"That's bullshit and you know it. I'm going inside and I'm going home with that guy."

"No!" he yells.

"Maybe I could depend on him. *He* wouldn't leave me when I needed him."

Ben drops his head and my heart breaks for him.

"I can't be what you want me to be, Bridget," he says softly.

"Yes, you can, Ben," she cries.

"I'm not wired like you!" he yells angrily.

The tears run down her face. "Like what? To be loved. To be happy?"

He doesn't answer.

"Is that the problem? I stupidly told you I loved you that night. Is that why you left me?"

Ben's face falls as if remembering, and he drops his head. He stands still and doesn't answer as he thinks.

I put my hand on my chest as my heart breaks for these two.

He looks up and, with renewed control, mutters the word, "Go."

She screws up her face. "What?"

"Go home with him."

Bridget's shoulders slump in defeat. "Ben," she sobs.

"Its not who I am Bridget. I can't be that man."

Bridget puts her head in her hands and starts to weep. Ben turns sadly and disappears inside. Max and I stand shocked as we watch him disappear into the darkness.

"Stupid prick," Max whispers.

"Natasha," Joshua calls me from behind and I turn and face my love. I'm so relieved that he and I don't go through this shit anymore.

"Bridget," Abbie calls as she comes round the corner in search for her friend.

"Take me and Didge home, boys." I walk over and grab Didge into an embrace. She is openly heartbroken. I look up the lonely, dark road to home.

Oh, man, what a shitty way to end a great night.

Adrian

I watch him slowly slide his hand down her clavicle, his tongue skimming along her jaw. "I'm taking you home," he breathes.

Abbie's eyes flicker with arousal and I smirk at Nicholas. Brock made his move as soon as his two sisters left. I had wondered how long it would take. This persona he has going on in front of the two of them is damn right humorous. They think butter wouldn't melt in his mouth but, boy, have I got news for them. They turn their eyes to me as they walk over and I look away, pretending I haven't been watching them make out for the last fifteen minutes against the wall.

"We are going to head off," states Brock, his eyes glance around. "Where's Cam?"

"He left with his friends."

Brock smirks and raises a brow. "He's in for a fun night."

"I guess." I smile.

Brock looks between Nicholas and I in question, then checks for the guards that are left. "You ok here, or shall I stay?"

"We're fine. Peter and Greg are at the bar."

"Ok." He checks his watch.

"What?" I frown.

"I might just stay for a bit."

I shake my head. "We are fine. You're not here to guard us."

His eyes flick to Abbie and she raises a a brow in question.

I smile. Abbie is good to go and somehow, I think Brock is in for a long night. The poor bastard's going to need painkillers tomorrow when she is finished with him.

Christ, Natasha and Didge are going to flip.

"We will leave after we finish these drinks," Nicholas replies to ease Brock's nerves.

He looks around again and then focuses back on Abbie, his eyes dropping down her body. She's as gorgeous as ever in a skin tight dress, and I can see him doing an internal risk assessment. Hmm, guard Adrian or go home and fuck a hot sex maniac? She wins. "Ok. Catch you both later," he replies.

Abbie bends and kisses me on the cheek. "Holy shit," she whispers in my ear.

I smile and Brock tugs her hard by the hand. "Hurry up, woman," he snaps.

She looks at me and smiles like the cat who got the cream as he drags her out, caveman style.

"That leaves us." Nicholas smiles.

My nerves start to thump. Time alone with Nicholas is dangerous. I just don't know how much longer I can resist him for.

His knowing eyes hold mine. "I have something to tell you."

I stare at him and sip my drink. "Ok."

"As you know I am flying out tomorrow."

I nod.

"What I haven't told you is where I'm going to."

I frown into my glass.

"I thought you would have asked me," he says, as though he is hurt.

"Where are you going, Nick?" I smile.

He hesitates. "I've taken a position lecturing at a University for twelve months."

My grin widens. "That's good."

"In London."

My face falls. No.

He grabs my hand over the table, clearly sensing my hurt.

I drop my head. I don't even know what to say to him. Go. Don't go. Why?

"I understand why you have pushed me away," he whispers.

My sad eyes meet his. That makes one of us then.

"I'm in love with you, Adrian."

My heart does a somersault and we sit still, staring at each other sadly. I have no words – nothing that will make sense, anyway.

"Why are you going then?" I can't stop myself from asking.

"Because… since I have been back and spent some time with you and your family…"

"They aren't my family."

"These people are your family, Adrian." He squeezes my hand. "They love you."

I smile sadly.

"I know what you need."

I frown. "What do I need?"

"You need to be loved wholeheartedly."

My heart sinks.

"And I can do that."

What is he saying? I don't understand.

"But I need more time."

I feel the lump in my throat start to hurt. He needs more time. Not 'I love you and I'm staying.'

I nod. "I know."

We sit still as our silence speaks volumes.

"He was a lucky man," I whisper. His eyes glaze over. "To have you love him so much."

"I love you, too. Babe. Please don't ever forget that."

"But," I whisper.

"But I'm not ready to give up his memory yet."

I nod as the tears fill my eyes. Stop it, for fuck's sake, stop it.

"I know you may not be here when I get back…" He hesitates as if the next sentence pains him. "You may meet someone else and fall madly in love."

"And then what?" I dare him to go on, angry that I'm so in love with someone who is emotionally unavailable.

"Then I will mourn the loss of you." His eyes hold mine. "It will be the biggest regret of my life."

Fury starts to pump through my blood. He's willing to take that risk. I sit still, unable to talk, unable to articulate what it is that I want to say. I don't even know what to think. I knew he wasn't ready and that's why I pushed him away. And now he is being totally honest and all I want to do is beg him to come back to me. Hell, this is one fucked up situation.

His eyes hold mine. "Say something," he begs.

I shake my head and stare at him through blurry eyes. "There's nothing to say Nicholas," I whisper through my hurt.

He grabs my hand again and lifts it up to kiss the back of it. "Can we stay in contact, please? I need to hear your voice."

I frown and rip my hand from his grip. What he is telling me is that he doesn't want me but wants to hold me on ice until he's ready.

"No," I reply coldly.

His face falls.

"Don't call me, don't visit me."

"Adrian, no," he whispers.

"Nick." I pause. "I can't be the reserve. I can't be the backstop. If you come back to me, come back to me with a full heart, not half a heart." My voice cracks as hurt pierces through my chest. "I deserve a full heart, Nicholas, because that's what I give."

His eyes tear up. "I know, babe."

I stand in a rush. "I'm leaving." I need to get out of here before I make a full-blown fool of myself and beg him to stay. I look around for Peter, where is he? I see him against the wall, signal that I'm leaving, and point to the door. He nods.

I leave the club in a rush and jump in a cab with Peter. I don't look back and I don't wait for Nicholas. My heart just couldn't bear it.

It's three am, I have been for a swim and am now in the shower. Nicholas' door was shut when I came in from the pool, so he must have come home and gone straight to bed.

I'm crushed, but also relieved at the same time. I did the right thing. I had regretted my decision to push him away, but he just confirmed what I knew all along. I wish I could talk to the girls. I think I might go next door and crawl into bed with Bridget. We can nurse our broken hearts together. I need to be with my people and lick my wounds.

The bathroom door opens and I turn. Nicholas stands amongst the steam in a pair of boxer shorts.

My breath catches but I don't cover up. I want him to see what he's missing out on. This body was his once.

He closes the door behind him and walks over to the shower. It's a walk in shower with no screen door and double showerheads.

His eyes drop, searching hungrily down my body, and I feel the pull of his arousal.

"Adrian," he whispers as his haunted eyes look straight through my soul.

I stare at him. "I need to say goodbye to you properly. He whispers."

I swallow the lump in my throat as my eyes drop to the obvious erection in his shorts.

He moves forward and his thumb brushes over my nipple and up to cup my face.

"Let me say goodbye, my love." He leans in and takes my lips in his. We kiss, slowly, his tongue tentatively meeting mine. "I need to say goodbye." He whispers again, and I feel the blood rush to my cock as my body goes into sensory overdrive. "I need you."

My eyes close. Oh God, I need him, too.

"Adrian, please. I'm begging, let me say goodbye to you."

That's it, I can't take it. I grab the back of his head, pull him into the shower and pin him up against the wall. We kiss almost violently, and I rip his shorts down his legs only to be rewarded with his huge, thumping penis stretching up against his stomach. His dark skin is rippled with muscles and my hand runs over his abs and down to his cock where I begin to stroke him hard. He hisses in approval as his hands drop to mine.

I need him, more than anything.

He wants to say goodbye to me then he's damn well going to remember it for a very long time. Never have I been with a man who is so perfectly, sexually suited. For ten minutes we kiss as if our lives depend on it until I can't take it. I need more and I need it now. I grab his head and push him down to his knees, his grateful dark eyes hold mine and a shudder runs through me just knowing the pleasure he is about to bestow on me. Nicholas Anastas is one hell of a lover.

With his big red lips, he takes me in his mouth and I grip the tiles to keep me on my feet. My head falls back in pleasure. God, he feels so fucking good, it's been too long since I've been in his perfect mouth. His tongue sweeps over the end of me before he bares his teeth.

"Fuck, I need you." He growls around me.

I rip his head back by the hair, bending down to kiss him violently. "Shut up and suck me."

CHAPTER 5

Natasha

IT'S SLIPPING.

The relief at being found alive, the elation to marrying my love, the mask. I feel as if I am locked in a room and poisonous gas is being slowly pumped in through a tiny hole, each hour that passes making it harder and harder to breathe, to carry on as normal. I look to Joshua who is naked and fast asleep next to me. My oasis in this desert. I love him so desperately.

Last night I woke to find him sitting in the chair next to our bed in total darkness, watching me silently. He didn't say anything. He didn't need to. I knew exactly how he felt and I'd held out my arms for him. He came to bed and we held each other tightly. It was as if the tighter we clung to each other, the further we could push the darkness away.

If only.

We are both playing the game, living the charade that all is well, neither one of us wanting to spoil our honeymoon for the other. We're refusing to let the trauma win.

My eyes go to the purple scar above his eyebrow. He didn't have that before I went missing. How did he get it? What has he been through?

My thoughts go to last night when Joshua and I took Didge

home after she fought with Ben. She was upset and crying, and it had been Joshua who took over the situation. He sat her up on the kitchen bench and made her tea. Mum heard us, got out of bed and came out to investigate and then he, Bridget and Mum sat on the kitchen bench while they drank tea and talked about anything except what had just happened. I stood silently in the corner as I watched their deflection. I felt as if I was hovering in the sky, witnessing them in the scene as they consoled each other over my death.

I close my eyes in pain, I hate what has happened to my family. I hate that they are so accustomed to deflecting pain that they do it without thinking. I get up to go to the bathroom and my thoughts cross to my precious sister, Didge. Her heart is broken, Ben doesn't want her, and yet I can't help but feel that somewhere deep down, he so desperately does. Why would he push such a beautiful soul away when I know that he loves her?

I look in the mirror at the scarecrow staring back at me and run my fingers through my lion mane of hair. I look terrible but I smirk anyway.

"Where are you, Presh?" Joshua calls out in half a panic.

"I'm here, baby," I answer from the bathroom.

"Oh, ok." He sighs as if relieved.

I walk out and fall into his open arms. He kisses my neck as he snuggles into me.

"Good morning, baby," I whisper into is hair.

"Morning, beautiful." He sighs contentedly. We lie still and he dozes back to sleep, but my thoughts keep wandering.

"Knock, knock." Bridget taps on the door, still in her pyjamas.

I smile when I see her. "Come in, Didge." I pat the bed next to me and she lays down beside me on top of the blankets.

"You ok?" I whisper.

"Yeah." She smiles sadly. "I think your drama queenism is rubbing off on me."

"I seriously doubt it. Nobody does it better than me."

"Tash?"

"Yes."

"I think I want to go home with Mum to Australia." She sighs

My heart sinks. I knew this was coming.

"Its ok, baby. You do what you need to do."

"I just don't think it's going to work with me and Ben."

I don't answer. I don't know what to say.

"I don't want to be around him. It just hurts." She sighs

"Why don't you stay with Adrian for a while? I know he would love to have you and then you won't see Ben. What are you going to do at home? What about the police?" I ask.

"I don't know." She sighs, defeated.

"I just..." I hesitate. "I hate the thought of being alone over there."

Her eyes hold mine. "Will you be ok?"

I smile.

"If I don't come back with you will you be ok in L.A. on your own?"

"Yes, I'm fine."

Her eyes hold mine and I can practically hear her brain ticking over.

I frown. "What?"

"Why are you so fine?"

I roll onto my back to escape her glare.

She sits up on her elbow to look at me. "Tash?"

"Stop it, Didge."

"I'm serious, Tash. You normally freak out if Joshua doesn't call you. How can you..." She stops herself as she tries to get the wording right in her head. "How can you go through what you have been through and be fine?"

I sit and jump over Joshua in a rush, and he wakes. "If you

came in here to annoy me, you are doing a good job," I stammer as I stand naked at the end of the bed in an outrage.

She lies calmly on her back and watches me.

"I'm serious, Natasha."

"Stop it." I stammer

"Why are you reacting like this? Why are you so angry? I just asked a question."

"Like what?" I yell.

"Not now, Bridget." Joshua snaps. "Don't upset her."

"I'm not trying to upset her. I want to hear about what she went through, I want to know how she escaped. I want to talk to my sister about her hurt."

"Get out." I cry.

Joshua sits up but can't get out of bed because he is naked underneath his sheet.

"Bridget!" he snaps.

"Joshua, stop it. She's acting weird. Why isn't she telling us anything and over analysing everything?"

My eyes fill with tears as I hear my heart beat in my ears. The tightening in my chest returns.

I storm into the bathroom and slam the door shut.

"Good fucking morning, Bridget," Joshua sneers. "We were having a nice lie in."

"Shut up," she hits back.

"Could you not let her wake up before you started that shit."

"Start my shit. Are you kidding? You are as bad as her. You nearly fucking killed yourself a week ago. You'd be dead if Nicholas hadn't put you into protective custody."

"Get out!" he barks.

I slam my hands over my ears and start to rock. Oh no. No. I close my eyes as panic starts to run through my bloodstream. Joshua nearly killed himself? Oh my god, I can't deal with this. I start to pace in the bathroom and shake my hands in a panic.

Calm down, calm down, just calm fucking down. I turn the shower on as hot as I can stand it, get in and slump to the floor as I try to slow my breathing. After roughly ten minutes, Joshua walks in and squats down next to the shower.

His worried eyes watch me and he puts his hand onto my knee. "You ok, Presh?" he asks gently.

I nod but don't answer.

"Are you going to stay in here for a while?"

I nod and put my hand over his on my knee.

"Do you want me to get you anything?"

I shake my head and he stays, just watching me.

"You're scaring me," he whispers.

I stare at him through blurry eyes, unable to answer. I'm scaring myself.

He gets in with me and wraps his arms around me and as we stand underneath the hot water for an extended time.

Eventually in the safe haven of my love's arms, I feel my stress begin to disappear.

Joshua

"Hello, can I speak to Nelson, please?" I ask Tiffany.

"Hello, Joshua," he answers. Nelson is my Human Resource Manager and I need him to follow something up for me.

"Hello, Nelson. I just wanted to thank you for your support over the last few months."

"That's ok, sir. I'm so happy that things turned out the way that they did."

I smile. "Me, too."

"Listen, I need you to do something for me," I tell him.

"Of course."

"I was in prison with a young man. I don't know his surname, but his first name was Jarvis."

He hesitates.

"He was in the cell opposite me and has been playing on my mind lately. He's very young, only just eighteen years old, I'd guess."

He hesitates again and I find myself smiling. This is one random phone call.

"I was wondering if you could ring the prison and find out more about him. Maybe see what his offenses are."

"Um, Mr. Stant—"

I cut him off. "If *you* can't get any details, ask the security team to do it for me."

"Ok. Why do you want these details, if I may ask?"

I shrug. "I'm not even sure yet. Let's see what he has done to get himself in prison first."

"Ok, sir. I will keep you posted."

"Thank you."

I hang up and blow out a long breath as my concentration is quickly stolen with thoughts of Natasha. How do I help her when I'm struggling myself? I have no idea how to navigate through this mess and work is the last thing on my mind.

Knock knock.

"Come in."

Brock walks into my office and takes a seat. "Hey," he says in his best carefree voice.

I sit back on my chair. "You know why I wanted to see you?"

"I do." He pauses.

I raise my eyebrows in frustration. "Well?"

"I've been thinking about it."

I roll my eyes. "Just fucking spit it out."

"I don't like the thought of working for you."

"You won't be working for me. The company would be yours."

"But I would know that it's really yours."

I shake my head. "Look if you don't want it then I will offer the deal to someone else. I don't give a fuck who does it. I want him caught and I thought with you know what you are doing, you would jump at the chance." I shrug my shoulders. "But obviously not." Fuck he pisses me off.

Brock holds up his hands in defence. "I'm not saying I don't want it, I'm saying I would like a loan for two years and then I'll pay you back."

My eyes hold his. "You want to pay me for the business?"

"Yes."

"Why?"

"Because I'm not taking hand outs from you."

I think for a moment. "Sounds fair."

"And I have one specification."

"What's that?"

"I want Jesten Miller to work for me."

"Fuck off. No. I won't stand for it."

"He would be good."

I glare at him. "He wouldn't fucking survive because I would kill the prick."

"Why, because he wants Natasha?"

"Just fucking shut up. I hated him even before he wanted my wife!"

He smirks. "You like saying that, don't you?"

"What?"

"My wife."

I smile. He's got me. I do say it a lot. "It has a certain ring to it, I have to admit."

He holds out his hand to shake. "So, it's agreed? I will pay you back in two years?"

I nod. "Deal."

"And Miller comes to work for me."

I shake my head. "No."

"You said it was my business."

"I'm not giving him one fucking cent."

"He knows Allender and he knows the case. He wants his accomplice caught as much as you do."

I think for a moment.

"You won't even fucking see him."

My eyes hold his. Fuck, I don't want that asshole anywhere near my family.

"He helped us when you were in prison, you know."

I roll my eyes. Cameron and Ben have already told me this.

"I didn't ask him to." I snarl.

"He did it for Natasha, not you." I narrow my eyes. "Just like he will find Allender's dodgy mate."

"Fucking hell," I snap. "I really don't want him around."

"Natasha is living in L.A. – he won't see her at all. Stop being a fucking baby."

I scrub my hands up and down my face in frustration.

Ben comes to the door. "Can I see you for a moment, Stan?"

My eyes flick to Brock. "Yes, we are done here."

"So, we have a deal?" He asks.

I blow out a breath in frustration. "All except Miller."

Brock's eyes flick to Ben. "Miller would be good working for me, don't you think?"

Ben nods in agreement. "Yes." He looks around nervously. "I wanted to speak to you together, actually."

I frown.

"Brock." Ben swallows as if nervous. "I would like to take up the job offer to come and work for you."

My face drops.

"Yes." Brock smiles.

"No." I snap.

"Joshua, I'm handing in my resignation. After everything that has happened, I just feel..."

"You are not going anywhere!" I snap. "This has to do with Bridget."

Ben drops his head.

"Why? What's going on with Bridget?" Brock snaps as his eyes flick between the two of us.

Oh, shit! He didn't know. Here goes that protective fucking brother act again.

"Nothing," Ben says with a snarl.

"Yeah, good. There better not be."

"Can you just get out?" I roll my eyes. "You are so fucking annoying."

"You are kind of fucking annoying yourself. I'm hiring Miller."

"No, you are not." I point to the door. "Get out."

"I'm ringing him now."

"Don't you dare." I snap.

My brow furrows as a thought crosses my mind. "Did you hook up with Abbie last night?"

He stills. "Possibly."

"And?" I question. Abbie has been the topic of many conversations in the past between Cam and Ben.

Brock winks mischievously.

My eyes meet Ben's. "I knew it." He smirks.

I shake my head. "Don't tell Tash and Didge. They will lose their shit." I sigh.

"Yeah I know. I told Abbs not to say anything."

"Good," I reply.

Ben smiles. "Cam's going to be filthy."

I laugh. "He so is. I haven't let him near her."

"Yeah, well, keep it up. Hes not having her." Brock snaps

I put my hands on my hips. God, this is going to end badly, but I don't care as long as it isn't my brother. My attention turns to Ben. "Take a seat, mate."

Brock goes to walk out. "Come and work with me Ben. Miller *is* coming," he calls over his shoulder.

"Out!" I bark, before I sit on the edge of my desk. "What's going on?"

Ben looks at the ground. "I think it's best if I resign."

"Best or easier?" He doesn't answer. "Why can't you make this work with Bridget. You care for her, right?"

"She deserves better."

I shake my head in annoyance. "That's not your decision to make. Ben, your old life is over. You need to let the past be the past and focus on the future."

"I don't see us working out in the long run."

"Why not?" I ask.

"We're too different."

I pause, knowing that's bullshit. "So, you are going to throw away your job, just because of some chick?"

"She's not just *some* chick," he warns me.

"That's not what you just said."

He rolls his eyes in frustration.

"You are contracted to me for another twelve months, and you *will* be fulfilling that contract."

He shakes his head in annoyance.

"Bridget is going to be staying with Murph. You can stay away from her if needs be."

He inhales in an attempt to stay calm.

I stare at him. "The paparazzi are going to go ape-shit when we get back and, between you and me, Tash is not doing so great. I need my team tight."

His eyes meet mine and he frowns. "Is she ok?"

I shrug. "I think it's just a time thing. I don't know."

"Anything I can do?"

"You can stay with me when I need you the most. We can look at your contract in twelve months but, right now, I do need you."

He gives one quick, curt nod. "Yes, ok." He stands and goes to walk out.

"Ben?" I call.

He turns back.

"She loves you." His eyes drop to the floor and I shake my head. "You're making a mistake, man."

"I'm doing this for her. My past will eventually catch up with me and she deserves better."

Natasha

Its mid afternoon and I lie on the lounge with my head on Joshua's lap. He's reading.

Nicholas comes to the front door and calls out. "Joshua."

"Come in, mate," he tells him.

He walks in and smiles. "Hello."

I sit up and smile brightly. "Hello."

His eyes dart around as if he is stuck for words and buying time. "I fly out tonight."

My heart drops. I was really hoping he wouldn't go.

"Where are you going?" asks Joshua.

"London."

Joshua's eyebrows rise in question.

"I'm lecturing in London. I agreed to it six months ago."

"How long for?" I ask.

"Twelve months."

My attention turns to Joshua as his head drops in frustration.

"What about Adrian?" I ask.

Nicholas fakes a smile. "I care deeply for Adrian, that won't change."

"Is that why you are leaving him?" Joshua asks flatly.

Nicholas shakes his head and blows out a breath. "It's a very long story."

Joshua and my eyes meet again. What is going on with every-one around here? First Ben, now Nick.

"I was just with Bridget," Nicholas says. Fucking snitch. What has she said? "She told me that you were upset this morning, Natasha."

"I'm fine," I reply.

He stays silent and stares at me while he thinks. His attention turns to Joshua. "I would like to speak to you two as a therapist for half an hour, if that's ok?"

Joshua glances at me. "We are doing fine, so that won't be needed."

Nicholas nods. "I know you are fine, and I know you are doing well, but as a friend who cares for you both, I feel I can't leave until I have hashed out a few things with you both."

"Nicholas," I sigh.

"Natasha, half an hour. That's all."

"It's not necessary," Joshua repeats.

An idea hits me. "Ok, half an hour, but I want to talk to you first."

He frowns. "About what?"

"About Adrian."

He rubs his forehead in frustration and drops into the high wing-back chair opposite.

"There is nothing to say about Adrian. He knows how I feel and he understands."

"How *do* you feel?" I ask.

He hesitates and glances at Joshua. Shit, I probably should do this privately.

"Joshua, can you leave us alone for ten minutes, please?" I ask.

Joshua frowns, clearly annoyed.

Nicholas holds up his hand. "No, he can stay, I have spoken to Joshua more than anyone about this, anyway."

"Where?" I frown.

"Prison," Joshua admits under his breath.

My face drops. "Oh." This is news. I turn my attention back to Nicholas.

He shakes his head as if making an internal decision to talk. "I don't know what's going on with me. I'm..." He hesitates. "I don't understand it myself. It's hard to explain."

I watch him for a moment. "Can I try and explain it for you and see if I'm close?"

His eyes roll and he holds out his hand, palm up, in defeat. "Be my guest."

"You are in love with Adrian." His eyes drop and he nods once. "And he's everything you could want in a partner."

He nods again.

"But, when you are with him, you feel as though Olivier is sitting in the corner watching the two of you together, listening to what you say to him, witnessing the love you make."

He continues to look at the floor to evade my gaze.

"And, likewise with Olivier, at night when you are alone, your thoughts used to be of him before you would go to sleep. Now Adrian's there, isn't he? You feel that, at times, when you want to think about Olivier and the love you shared, you find yourself missing Adrian and you want him with you so you can hold him close."

Joshua becomes uncomfortable and sits back, rubbing his hand through his hair.

"So, effectively, you are in love with two men and you feel like you are cheating on them both. Each moment with one makes you think of the other."

His haunted eyes meet mine.

"When you're with Adrian, you know Olivier is watching and when your mind is on Olivier... you're missing Adrian."

"I can't take it anymore," He whispers as he drops his head.

"So you are going to be alone?" I ask flatly.

"Adrian deserves better. How could I tell him I feel guilty for loving him? It's not fair."

"You deserve better, too, Nicholas. Why can't you love them both?"

"Because what happens when I…" He stops, looking up at me.

"When you die?" I ask, surprised. He drops his head again. "You are worried that when you die you will have to make a choice between your two loves, is that it?"

He shakes his head. "I don't know what I think anymore."

I haven't got an answer for that. Nobody knows what happens when we die. I need to change my tactic. "Ok, let me ask you this. What if Olivier hand picked Adrian and sent him to you." He doesn't look at me. "What if all he wants is for you to be happy with someone who loves you just as much as he did."

He stands and goes to look out the window.

"You have to forgive yourself, Nicholas, and be prepared to have two men with you at all times. You have to learn to deal with it because you and I both know neither of them is going anywhere."

He stays silent, thinking.

"You are not forgetting Olivier by loving Adrian. You are not betraying Adrian by thinking of Olivier. The only person you are hurting is yourself."

He turns and smiles despite his glazed eyes. "You should maybe think of a career in Psychology."

I grin. "Nah, I got enough of my own shit going on."

My eyes find Joshua who is smiling proudly.

Nicholas seemingly pulls himself together. "Lets talk about you two."

I smile at Joshua and take his hand. Weirdly, talking about someone else's problem has made me feel better.

"How are things physically between you?"

Joshua raises his eyebrows in horror and glances at me.

"I'm here as a doctor, not a weird friend." He smirks.

"Excellent." I smirk.

Joshua raises a single eyebrow in jest. "Excellent?" He mouths proud of himself.

"That's great." Nicholas smiles.

"Sexual malfunction is common in PSTD."

Joshua frowns. "PSTD?" he asks.

"Post traumatic stress disorder."

"Nope, we don't have that," Joshua tells him, relieved. "We definitely don't have that."

My stomach sinks a little, I might have.

"And the communication between you two?" Nicholas asks.

"It's fine," Joshua replies a little too quickly.

Nicholas' eyes hold Joshua's. "So, you have discussed with her the information that was presented in court, along with your desire to end your life in prison?"

Joshua's head drops and my eyes close in pain.

"And Natasha, have you told Joshua anything about what happened to you in that room?"

I don't answer, simply staring straight ahead.

"How you escaped?"

I drop my head and my anxiety starts to rise.

"What you had to do to survive?"

I shake my head softly.

"Natasha, you know more than anyone that you need to talk and you need to vent, write down all your feelings. Writing in a diary is your coping mechanism. Why haven't you been doing that?"

I stare at him for an extended time. I want to answer, I really do, but the lump in my throat is blocking my voice.

"Why, Natasha?"

The tears form behind my eyes.

"I need you to vocalise it for me so I understand – so that Joshua understands."

I drop my head again and Joshua wraps his arm around me. "Look, this is too much," Joshua warns him. "I don't want her getting upset."

"And why is that Joshua? Why do you feel you have to walk on eggshells around Natasha?"

Joshua frowns. "Why do you fucking think?"

Nicholas turns to Joshua. "How has everything been with you?"

"Fine," he replies defiantly.

"So, you are off your sleeping medication?"

Joshua doesn't answer and my eyes rise to his in question. "What?"

Joshua rubs his hands through his hair in frustration. "I'm just having trouble sleeping, that's all. It means nothing."

"What do you think about when you're awake at night?"

"Nothing."

"Nothing at all?"

"Nope."

"I think I know what you think about. Natasha got taken on your watch."

Joshua's cold eyes stare at Nicholas.

"It was your fault she nearly died. It was your fault that Amelie did this. It was your fault Natasha had to go through this."

Joshua stands swiftly.

"She was your fiancé. You should have protected her."

"Shut up," Joshua whispers coldly.

"This is all your fault. Isn't that right, Joshua?"

"Yes!" he snaps. "Of course it's my fucking fault."

I shake my head as tears pool to blur my vision. "No, baby, this wasn't your fault."

"Yes, it was." Joshua sucks in precious air into his lungs as he tries to calm himself down.

"We will come back to this in a moment." Nicholas smiles sympathetically.

He turns his attention back to me. "I have an assignment for you, Natasha."

I like assignments, I smile. "Ok."

"I would like you to go back and fill in your diary for me. Tell me about what happened when you were taken, day by day."

My face falls and I shake my head.

"Why not?"

I stay silent.

"I…" I hesitate. "I don't." I stop as the tears start to run down my face and the lump in my throat hurts me.

"Why, Natasha. I would like you to give me a reason."

"I can't."

"Why not?"

"I'm scared," I whisper.

"You don't want to go back there."

I shake my head quickly.

"It was terrible, wasn't it?"

I nod sharply.

"Its better not to think about it, isn't it?"

I nod again.

"You know how we talked about me needing to learn to live with being in love with two men?" Joshua and I both nod. "I need you two to learn to live with something, too. You need to acknowledge what has happened to the both of you. You need to acknowledge that you have both survived a life-changing event. You're different people now."

Joshua drops his head sadly.

"And that's ok! It's ok to be slightly damaged version of yourselves."

My eyes meet Joshua's and I grab his hand.

"It's ok to be imperfect. It's ok to have down days and bad memories."

I stare at him through my tears.

"What's not ok, is pretending that it didn't happen."

I nod and Joshua drops his head.

"You two have a bond. You've both been through so much, yet you survived."

Joshua smiles and puts his arm around me, softly kissing my forehead as I wipe my tears away.

"Rely on each other. Talk to each other. Support each other."

Joshua nods. "We will."

I smile but the tears won't stop. I lean forward and pull a tissue from the box, blowing my nose loudly.

Nicholas smiles. "You two are going to be fine. You just have to be kind to one another and let yourselves have a moment of weakness every day. If you keep acting tough all the time, you're going to crash and burn."

I nod, smile and hold out my hand, grateful when Nicholas takes it in his.

"Thank you," I whisper.

"You *are* going to be ok," he repeats.

"I know."

Nicholas stands and pulls me into an embrace and we stay there for a moment.

"Come back for my friend," I whisper.

CHAPTER 6

LOUNGING ON THE day bed by our pool, Adrian lies across me with his head high on my stomach. Bridget and Abbie are sprawled down the other end as we all stare at the sky. The mood is sombre with two of my friends down and out.

"What did he say at the airport?" Bridget frowns. Adrian took Nicholas to the airport last night, and we are catching up on the goodbye activities.

"That he loved me. That he would stay if he could." He sighs sadly.

"What a load of shit," Abbie snaps.

"I know, right?"

"Why is he fucking leaving then?" Abbie snorts.

"Just wait to see if you hear from him," Bridget replies softly as she puts her hand reassuringly on Adrian's foot to reassure him.

"He rang me when he landed, then again this morning."

"What did he say?" I ask.

"I didn't answer."

"Oh, man," I reply sadly.

"I'm looking forward to getting home this week, actually," Adrian murmurs.

I feel my stomach flip. I wish I was as excited. I'm dreading it.

"Guys, about that..." Abbie sits up onto her elbows to look at our faces.

"I think I'm going home to Australia."

"Why, Abbs?" I frown, where is this coming from?

She shrugs. "I'm homesick. I miss my…" she hesitates.

"What?" Bridget pushes.

"My Tristan."

I roll my eyes. Army guy. God, get off it. She hooked up with Brock two days ago.

"You don't seem to be missing him," I reply deadpan.

Adrian smiles and holds his hand back over his head for me to high five and I slap my hand against his.

"What are you referring to?" she asks, annoyed.

"Um, Brock. What else would I be referring to? He is our brother, in case it slipped your mind," I answer coldly.

She puts her hands over her face in shame. "I thought you didn't know."

"We don't want to know," Bridget snaps. "How could you?"

"H-how could I not?" she stammers. "It just happened."

"Is he why you are leaving?" Adrian asks.

She blows out a defeated breath. "I just want to go home and–"

Adrian cuts her off. "What about your finger prints?"

"As if I am going to get fingerprinted."

"You might," I warn her.

"Ben said the case has gone cold. Please remember this was a prostitute who was bribing copious amounts of men. They don't finger print you for traffic offenses and I'm sure as shit not going to get arrested."

We all stay silent for a moment.

"I have already asked Victoria, and we are going to take a commercial flight together on Friday."

I frown. "You're serious. You're actually going?"

"What have I just been saying? Do you fucking listen to me at all?"

"Not if we can help it," Adrian mutters.

I smile, my hand falls to the top of his head and I run it mindlessly through his hair.

"Didge, you can stay with me," states Adrian.

Bridget eyes the two of us. "I don't want to impose."

"You are not an imposition. I would love to have a housemate for a while."

"Really?" She smiles as she rubs her hand on his foot. "I want to go home, too, if I'm honest, but I want to wait until Tash is feeling better."

My stomach sinks. I want to tell her that I'm fine, but I'm trying to take Nicholas advice to stop pretending. And besides, the longer I drag out Didge staying with me, the more chance she has to patch things up with Ben.

Joshua comes out the back glass doors. "Murph, the scanner is broken," he calls.

We all look over to him standing with both hands on his hips. "Yeah, so?" Adrian answers.

Joshua frowns. "So… do you know how to fix it?"

"How would I fucking know how to fix it?" Adrian sighs. "You're the computer geek."

Joshua blows out a frustrated breath and I smile to myself. Adrian is clearly not in the mood for taking shit today.

"Ben has one in his office," Adrian calls.

Joshua turns and goes back inside, returning moments later with the papers he has to scan. "Don't mind me," he says sarcastically. "You keep lying there with your head on my wife's tits."

"Ok," replies Adrian.

I give Joshua a cute little wave and a smile, but he shakes his head, unimpressed, and keeps walking.

"What happened with Nicholas the other night?" Abbie suddenly asks.

Adrian shrugs.

Abbie sits up to look him in the eyes. "You blew his mind, didn't you? Please, tell me you blew that stupid prick's mind."

Adrian smiles broadly. "I gave him a night that he won't forget in a hurry, put it that way."

I smile and pat him on the forehead. "Good boy," I whisper. We all fall silent again as we think.

"I think he will come back for you, Adrian," I offer quietly.

Adrian sits up. "Yeah, well, I'm not going to be here. This was his last chance."

My stomach drops. Oh no.

"Didge and I are going on a man hunt when we get back. We are sick to fucking death of being fucked over."

"Amen," Bridget cries.

"Maybe I should stay then." Abbie scoffs. "Sounds like the fun might just be about to begin."

Joshua

I sit in the darkened room as I watch her, the weight sits heavily on my shoulders and my mind refuses to stop. She still has the marks from past bruises on her and I can't let it go. I need to know how she got them.

Natasha wakes with a start. "Joshua," she croaks out, realising I'm not in bed with her.

"I'm here, Presh," I answer softly from my chair in the darkened corner.

Her face falls. "Are you ok?"

I nod sadly.

She watches me for a moment. "Did you take your sleeping tablets?"

"Yes."

She looks to the clock on the side table. It's 2:30 a.m. "You only get four hours from them?"

"Yes."

She sits up. "Joshua, come back to bed, baby."

I stand and sit next to her and she cups my cheek in her hand.

"You look so sad, so lost. What are you thinking about, my love?" she asks.

I stare at her for a moment. "Did he use his hand to hit you?" I whisper.

She swallows and nods once.

Pain lances through my chest. I can't bear that she went through this because of me.

"How often, how often did he..." I stop, unable to go on.

"How often did he hit me?" she finishes for me.

"Yes."

"When I didn't do what he wanted me to do."

What he wanted her to do? It never even occurred to me before. Oh my God. I feel like I can't breathe and bile rises from my stomach.

"Did he...?" I hesitate again. I can't even say it out loud.

"Rape me?" she whispers.

I drop my head and screw up my pained face as tears fill my eyes.

"No." She sits up and cups my cheek once more.

"He would have as soon as he got the go ahead. Amelie protected me to an extent."

"Don't say that. It was me that should have protected you," I whisper. "This was all *my* fault, Natasha. *I* should have protected you. *I* should have picked up that Amelie was unstable."

She leans in and kisses me gently, trying to calm me. "I'm ok, Joshua. I survived. I wasn't raped. How could you have possibly known?"

"How hard did he hit you?"

She hesitates and frowns as her eyes mist over. "He only hit me really hard twice with his fists. He knocked me out once. Mostly he would slap me until I fell and then kick me when I was on the ground."

I scrunch my eyes closed. I can't bear this. "You should have killed him," I whisper.

Her eyes hold mine for a moment. "The scary thing is, Josh, I wished I killed him, too."

I watch her struggle with her internal thoughts.

"What are you thinking?" I ask.

Her dark eyes meet mine. "I can still feel the way the glass felt as it sliced though his neck. I can still hear him screaming out in pain."

I swallow. "What memory is stronger? Him hitting you or you attacking him?"

"Me attacking him is much stronger."

"Good," I whisper. "I don't want you to remember the other stuff. You need to try and forget it, baby."

"Can you tell me? Can you tell me about the night I went missing?"

"Why would you want to hear that shit?" I murmur.

She frowns. "I..." Then she hesitates. "I'm trying to fit the puzzle pieces together. I think it will help me."

I lay down and pull her across my body so her head is on my arm and her top leg is thrown over mine. My hand runs aimlessly through her hair.

"How did you find I was gone?" she whispers.

I frown as I remember. "I was cold. It was so cold. I could hear the wind banging on something."

She, too, frowns as she tries to visualise my words. "What time was this?"

"Dawn. It was foggy."

She lies still as she listens.

"I thought you were in the bathroom and I went back to sleep. I could have saved you, but I went back to sleep."

"Josh," she whispers.

"The door kept banging and eventually it woke me up completely. I went looking for you."

"Oh Josh. My heart aches for you," She whispers. "I can't imagine going through this."

I hesitate; knowing the next part of the story is what upsets me. I can't bear going back there. The lump in my throat forms and my chest tightens.

"Then what happened?" she prompts.

"I slipped."

"You slipped?" she repeats.

I nod.

"God, Josh, your heart rate is racing. You're back there, aren't you? You relive this every night?" she whispers in horror.

My eyes mist over.

"Did you hurt yourself?"

"Huh?"

"When you slipped?"

"No," I reply blankly.

"Was the deck wet?" she asks.

"I slipped on your blood."

She gasps.

"There was blood everywhere," I whisper.

She screws up her eyes in pain.

I feel perspiration start to wet me.

"There was so much blood and..." I hesitate as I realise that this might upset her further.

"Tell me," she urges. "I'm ok and I want to hear this, Joshua."

"There were drag marks in your blood, at the side of the boat."

She closes her eyes in pain. "Holy fuck. This is horrific, no wonder you aren't sleeping."

I remain still, numb as the horror seeps through my body.

"What did you do?" she asks softly.

"I started to yell for you. I-I couldn't find you."

Her tears start to fall like a burst dam.

"Ben came."

She frowns. "Where was Ben?"

"He heard me screaming."

She closes her eyes again.

"We were diving under the water."

"Josh," she whispers. "It's ok. I'm here, baby, I'm here." She pulls me closer.

I shake my head. "But I couldn't find you." My voice is strained. "Joshua."

"I couldn't remember, Natasha. I still can't remember. I can't stand the thought that I don't remember something so significant."

"It's ok, Joshua, you were drugged."

"No, it's not ok. I should have protected you. I-I should have been able to protect you." I stammer as my stress hits a new level.

She kisses my chest. "I'm alive. Everything is ok."

We lie still for an extended time, both lost in our own thoughts.

"Tell me about prison." She kisses my chest.

"It's cold," I reply flatly.

"What do you mean?"

"I would shiver at night because I was so cold."

"Nicholas said you wanted to end your life when you were in there. Is that true?"

I'm still, deathly still as I relive the grief all over again. The lump in my throat hurts to swallow.

"It was a very dark time for me, Tash. I can't explain how low I was."

"Do you still have dark thoughts?

"No," I reply without hesitation.

"I'm here, baby. I will never let you go."

We cling onto each other so tightly, trying desperately to chase our demons away, and I know I need to escape this heavy feeling that hangs over me. I need to learn how to forget.

Natasha

"It's 4:00 p.m. and the day has been long. I'm exhausted and we have hardly slept. Joshua and I talked for hours last night. He's been to Hell and back. All the honesty eventually broke me down and I cried for hours.

I killed a woman.

I killed a woman I knew and I now realise that I have no idea how to deal with it. I feel like I should feel guilty, but I'm just relieved that I escaped. Joshua was furious when I finally opened up about Carl hitting me. He said he wished I had killed the monster. The sick thing is... I kind of wish I had, too. What kind of person have I turned into?

"Where do you want to live, Tash? We need to discuss this," Joshua asks me.

I frown into the spaghetti on toast I am eating and I drag my hand down over my face in frustration. "I don't know."

"Do you want to go back to L.A.?"

"Yes." I frown. "I told you I want to be close to Adrian, Cam and Didge. Did I tell you that Abbie is going home to Australia?"

"Ben told me."

My eyes hold his. "Do you think that's a good idea?" I ask.

He shrugs.

"What does that mean?"

"It means I don't know," he answers curtly.

I smirk. My man is tired and cranky like a child. Some things never change.

"I think maybe you're right and we should get an apartment for a while."

His eyes hold mine. "You don't want to go home to our house?" he asks.

"No." I stand and take my plate back to the sink. "I don't think I ever will."

He watches me but remains silent.

"People were in our house, Joshua, and we were filmed in our bed. There is no bigger invasion of privacy than that."

He stays quiet as he thinks. We've never discussed this before, and even though I know he knows, he has never once asked about what was on the footage from our house.

"What did you see?" He replies.

That angry burn starts to scorch through my veins. "I watched us have sex in every damn position possible."

He stays watching me.

"How many people do you think have watched the tapes?" I snap.

He purses his lips.

'The police, Amelie, her helpers." I raise an eyebrow.

His eyes drop.

"Anal."

His eyes flick back up to mine.

"Yes, Josh. We were filmed having anal sex. We were filmed in every derogatory position you can imagine and it's forever burned into my brain."

"For fucks sake." He growls as he runs his hands though his hair angrily.

"Can we stay at the hotel we stayed at when we got broken into for a little while when we get back?" I ask.

"Yes, of course," he mutters, lost deep in thought.

Thunder claps loudly and my eyes drift to look out of the window. It's getting dark and cloudy outside. My mind goes back to me walking in the forest after I escaped during the time before the impending storm. I was so desperate to find shelter before the rain started. The dark forest was so unwelcoming and I kept staring up at the sky, willing it to hold off. A cold chill runs down my spine as the memory becomes too real, too raw.

Stop it. It's over.

It's so cold. I walk into my bedroom and retrieve a woollen blanket from the end of our bed, wrapping it around me for protection. I'm hoping that by warming myself up it's going to make the memory of being cold and petrified leave me. It thunders again and I sit down on the end of the lounge, bringing my feet up in front of me. Please, stop. Please don't rain. My heart rate starts to pick up and my anxiety rises.

Joshua watches me. "You ok?" He frowns.

"I'm just tired," I reply too quickly.

"We will have an early dinner and turn in."

"Yes."

The thunder rumbles loudly and I jump. I get a flash of me sitting on the bed in the dark with a gun, staring out the window as the lightning flashed. The rain is hitting the window and my feet are hurting. I'm wearing clothes that are way too big and smell of camphor. I stand and walk to the bedroom. I need to get away from all of this.

More thunder.

I see myself breaking the glass with a rock to get into that house. I inhale deeply. God, stop it.

I sit on the end of the bed and close my eyes. Calm down, calm down. The heavy raindrops start to fall, and I feel my anxiety rise further.

"Natasha?" Joshua asks quietly as he comes after me. "Are you ok?"

"Yes, I'm fine," I snap. Just leave me a fucking lone.

"Do you want a cup of tea?"

I nod. "Yes, please." He walks back into the kitchen and the rain comes down – heavy torrential rain – and I feel tears swell in my eyes. The vision of waiting in that tin shed with a gun in the pouring rain takes over me. I hate this. I hate seeing this. Make it stop.

"Here."

I look up in surprise to see Joshua is back with my tea already. I go to take it, but my hand is shaking.

Joshua watches my hand for a moment. "You are getting a migraine." His voice is soft and caring.

I drop my head.

It continues to pelt down with rain and I scrunch up my face in pain as the vision of Amelie standing in front of me fills my head.

Joshua drops to sit next to me on the bed. "What is it, baby?"

I'm holding the gun at her and she's goading me. I close my eyes to try and block it out.

"Tash, what's wrong? Tell me what's wrong."

I shake my head and screw up my face. "I'm so sorry."

"For what?"

"I didn't mean to hurt her."

Joshua wraps his arms around me. "Ssh."

The lightning crashes again and I jump in his arms.

"Its ok, baby. Its ok," he whispers.

I start to cry uncontrollably against Joshua's chest as he holds me.

"You don't have the guts." Amelie sneers in my mind.

I feel myself lose control and pull the trigger three times.

She falls to the ground bleeding and my tortured eyes meet Joshua's.

"I killed her." I sob. "She died because of me."

The noisy rain comes down and I cry even harder. "M-make it stop," I stammer.

"Make the rain stop."

"Baby, let's get into the shower," Joshua whispers.

I nod nervously.

"Natasha," I hear Cameron yell from the front door.

"In here," Joshua calls out.

Cameron walks in and his face drops. He sits on the other side of me on the bed. "Are you ok, babe?" he asks.

"No, she's not," Joshua answers for me.

"It's the rain," Cameron whispers.

"Huh?"

"It's the rain. It's making me think of it, too."

"What do you mean?" Joshua asks.

"It was raining heavy for days when Natasha was running and hiding. The day with the…" He stops midsentence, unsure what to say.

Joshua squeezes me to his chest just that little bit harder.

"Make it stop, Cam," I whisper through my tears.

The lightning crashes and I lose control, slapping my hands over my ears as I cower and curl into Joshua with fright.

"Jesus." He holds me tight.

The lightning cracks again, and I cry out loud, holding my hands over my ears.

"Give her something!" Joshua snaps.

"Like what?"

"A fucking sedative."

"I do have her migraine medication with me in case she needed it," he replies.

I begin to cry out loud.

"Christ," Cameron mutters as he stands.

"Fine. Hurry up."

The last thing I remember is Cameron giving me a needle and Joshua carrying me to the shower. I fall into an almost zombie state as my brain tries to shut out the horror.

"It's ok, Presh. I'm here. I've got you, baby."

The horror of post-traumatic stress lives within me. I am sombre and I'm tired. I don't now where I want to be, but I know it isn't here, dealing with this.

The trip from the airport to the hotel our temporary home in L.A. – is made in complete silence. It's 1am and Ben, who is driving, has just had an altercation with a photographer at the airport. He was only trying to protect me. The photographer tried to grab me to get his shot when Ben lost it, pushed him, sending the photographer flying until he fell over.

They will try and sue him, they always do.

Is this our new life?

Paparazzi will go into overdrive with the news that we have returned and will all be waiting for the first shots. What a mess. Joshua is wound up and nobody is speaking. After my little breakdown on Tuesday, I spent the next two days in bed with Cameron and Joshua fussing over me. Trying to will me back to life.

It worked… just.

Joshua has insisted that Cameron goes and stays with Adrian and Bridget for a few days. Cameron is struggling, too, and I know my husband is concerned for his beloved brother. We have all noticed that he hasn't been his carefree self since we have been in Kamala. Cameron's mind is preoccupied with regret. Could we have saved Amelie if we had done things differently? We will never get the chance to know now, and I think that's half the battle: the feeling of helplessness we all share.

The finality of the situation.

We pull into the round driveway and Joshua leads me out of the car where an attendant is waiting.

"Mr. Stanton, this way." He gestures with his hand to the elevator. Joshua and I nod gratefully. A long check in would be unbearable at this stage of the night. Two minutes later, and on the tenth floor, we follow the attendant down the corridor, eventually spotting our security all standing outside the doors to their apartments. I nod a silent thank you for their support.

"Hello."

They smile as we walk past.

The porter opens the door of the room we had last time. I look in and smile, I have happy memories here and a certain hot kind of massage runs naked through my mind.

Joshua nods. "Thank you."

The attendant hands over two key cards.

"Nobody can access this level though the lifts?" Joshua asks.

"No, sir. All access has been blocked and the fire stairs are locked from the other side."

"We will have a guard on the front doors at all times," Joshua instructs.

My heart sinks and I know my life will be different forever.

"Of course." The attendant nods nervously.

"Thank you." Joshua nods back.

"If there is anything else, sir, please call this number directly." He hands over a business card with his personal details on it.

Joshua nods and holds his hand out in a *get out of my fucking room* gesture, and I bite my bottom lip to contain my smile.

Joshua closes the door, turns to me and takes me in his arms.

"I think I need to give my girl a massage."

I inhale his scent. "Yes, Mr. Stanton. Yes, you do."

Joshua

"Yes," I answer my phone. We have been back in L.A. for three weeks and I am in work mode.

My eyes drift to Cameron who is lying on the lounge in my office, skimming through his phone.

"Hello, Mr. Stanton. The keys have arrived from the real estate."

"Thank you, Tiffany. I'll collect them from you shortly."

Adrian walks in with a bundle of papers and starts to rearrange them to file away.

"Tell me about this guy again?" Cameron asks as he sits up onto his elbow.

"He's a kid, only just eighteen." Adrian sighs.

I blow out a breath, this could be the most stupid thing I have ever done.

"So, let me get this straight. You meet some scummy kid in prison, and now you are giving him a job, an apartment and a car?" Cameron shakes his head in disgust.

"Yep, pretty much."

"Don't leave your wallets laying around, this is going to end fucking badly. You will come in one morning and your whole office will be cleaned out." He smirks, clearly amused.

I sit back in my chair. "It could."

"Why did you want me here? I don't want to meet him."

"Because I want you to help me with him."

"The fuck I am." He groans. "I want nothing to do with fucking criminals."

I frown and inhale in frustration. "I think he's a good kid, he just hasn't had any opportunities."

"What happened to you in prison? What are we, a fucking charity now?"

"No. Look, if he does one thing wrong, he goes back in. I paid his bail, I'm giving him a chance and if he fucks it up, I won't make excuses for him."

Adrian and Cameron look at each other, concerned. "He's going to have to work hard. This isn't a free ride."

"What's his name?" Adrian sighs.

I pick up the release papers on my desk and flick through them. "Jarvis."

Adrian pouts. "Cool name." He raises his eyebrows as if surprised.

I smirk.

Adrian narrows his eyes. "What is *that* look for?"

I shrug. "You two make out you are so gangster, but when it comes down to it, you're both as soft as shit."

"Fuck off," Cameron mutters as he goes back to his phone. "I'm the king of gangster."

"You still good for tonight?" I ask Cameron.

"Yes." He sighs, annoyed.

Adrian and I smile at each other.

"And you will have to be there early to let them in."

"I fucking know. Jesus Christ, you owe me some shit."

I smile. "Thank you."

A knock rings against the door. "Come in," I yell.

Ben appears first, the small boy behind him looks petrified.

I smile and hold my hand out to shake his. "Jarvis, we meet again."

He smiles. "Hey, fuck off."

"Watch it." Ben growls.

I smile at the private joke we have before my attention turns to Ben. "It's ok, that's what he calls me."

Adrian's face drops in horror. "Why would you call him that?"

The kid shrugs "Because those were the only two words he ever said in prison."

The boys' eyes all meet and they shake their heads and smile. "My apologies for not picking you up myself but I didn't want to go back to that place. This is Cameron, my brother, and Adrian is the manager here." He shakes their hands and tries to smile. He's as nervous as hell. Poor kid. "And you know Ben, the head of my security."

He turns to Ben and nods.

"Take a seat." I gesture to the chair.

He falls into it, completely nervous. He's wearing old clothes and appears un-kept. My eyes sweep over him. "Take a seat, Ben."

Ben sits down next to Jarvis.

"I want to know why you went to prison." I already know this but I want him to tell me.

He drops his head. "Stealing cars."

I nod. "Why did you steal cars?"

He swallows nervously. "I had my reasons."

My eyes hold his. "So, you used to steal cars, but in prison you gave up a million dollars to get me heroine when I asked you for it?"

He doesn't answer me.

"Jarvis, I knew you could get it, so why didn't you?"

He shrugs and looks to the floor.

I see Cameron and Adrian make eye contact with each other as they have light bulb moment as to why I want to help him.

"You even went so far as to tell the warden I wanted to kill myself and got me moved to protective custody. Why?"

He doesn't answer.

"If you were so hard up for money, why did you do that?" I ask. "I really do want to know."

"I knew you would regret it."

My eyes hold his, but he looks away.

I swivel in my chair. "I have a business proposition for you."

"I'm good. Thanks anyways." He starts to stand.

"Sit down," Ben orders. He falls nervously back into his chair.

"Let me rephrase that. You were going to be in prison for another two years, but now that I have paid your bail, you will do whatever I ask of you for two years."

He looks at me, stone faced.

"You will work here at the office for me as a trainee. Nothing too hard at first, and we will help you with everything. I have rented you an apartment and we'll go and get you a car tomorrow."

He frowns.

My eyes drift to Adrian and then down at his clothing. "Adrian will go with you shopping this afternoon and buy you a new wardrobe."

"This isn't necessary."

"Yes, it is." I reply.

"You looked after me and now I am going to look after you, whether you like it or not."

"I don't fit in here."

"I don't care. You will in time. You are to leave that old life and those old friends behind you, or I will take you back to prison myself and you will have everything taken from you."

His wild eyes hold mine and I can see that he's angry. I smile on the inside. I like this kid.

"You will be given a guard of your own at all times.

He frowns in disgust. "I don't need a fucking security guard!" he snaps.

I raise an eyebrow. "I know you don't, he's there so I know you are sticking to the rules. No crime, no seediness. New life."

He runs his hands through his hair.

"I'm giving you an opportunity, Jarvis, to turn your life around. I want you to take it with both hands."

He glares at me.

I stand and smile proudly. "Let's go and see your new apartment."

He frowns. "You got me an apartment? You are serious?"

I nod. "Deadly."

Adrian smiles sympathetically. "I think we should go clothes shopping first, Jarvis."

The kid looks down at his clothing. "What's wrong with my clothing?"

Arian looks to the ceiling for guidance. "Everything."

Ben pulls the car into the parking lot, pops the hood, and we start to retrieve the multiple shopping bags from the trunk. Adrian is hiding his excitement but I know poor Jarvis is his new styling victim. We have just bought almost everything in town.

"Its up here." Adrian signals to the block of apartments to the right.

Jarvis stops and looks at the building in awe. I drop my head to hide my smile. He has been silent throughout the afternoon, but polite. I wish I knew what was going through his mind. We finally get to the third floor and Adrian shuffles around for his key before handing it to Jarvis.

Jarvis puts his bags onto the floor and looks at the key in his hand. I smile and gesture to the door with my chin as I struggle with the bags of shopping. "Hurry up, fuck you."

He hunches his shoulders, opens the door, and peers in like a scared child.

"Go in," Adrian urges.

He slowly enters and we follow him and drop all the shopping on the floor. He stands in the foyer wringing his hands nervously as he looks around.

"Do you like it?" Adrian asks.

He nods quickly.

I put my hands on my hips and look around. This *is* pretty nice, actually, Adrian has had it furnished in chocolate and cream colours. A large plasma screen is on the wall and a glass coffee table sits in the middle of the room. The kitchen is modern, black, and marble, while the dining table is the same glass as the coffee table in the lounge room.

"Over here is your bedroom." Adrian disappears up the hall. We follow and find a large master suite with a bathroom.

Jarvis eyes widen. "This is the bedroom?" he whispers.

"Yep," Adrian replies proudly. "Oh, come and see the kitchen."

We follow him back out to the kitchen and he opens the pantry door. "I had groceries delivered this morning. I didn't know what you liked to eat so just eat what you like and the other stuff can go to waste."

Jarvis pulls out the crisper and looks at all of the vegetables.

I frown. "Do you know how to cook, Jarvis?"

"Umm." His scared eyes search all around.

"Oh, and I got you cable." Adrian walks into the lounge room and holds up the remote at the television, switching on the music.

Jarvis stands at the kitchen bench quietly as he looks around. He's so overwhelmed.

"Welcome to your new home, mate." I smile.

His scared eyes meet mine and he shakes his head. "I..." He swallows. "I don't belong here."

I shrug my shoulders. "Tough, 'cause this is where you are living."

Adrian smiles and pours himself a *Diet Coke* from the fridge. "Want a drink, anyone?" He holds up the bottle.

We both nod and take the glasses from Adrian.

"I will get your things transported here. Just write down your current address and we will organise everything."

Jarvis' eyes drop to the floor. "That won't be necessary," he murmurs.

"Why not?" I ask.

He shrugs. "I don't really have anything."

I roll my lips and look to Murph who shrugs, also.

"Where is your home?" Murph asks as the room falls silent.

"I don't have a home."

I frown.

"I'm a ward of the state – a foster kid. I've never had a permanent home."

My eyes stay glued to him as my stomach drops.

Adrian puts his hand on his chest sympathetically. "How did your parents die?" Adrian asks gently.

He shrugs again. "Don't know and don't care. On the end of a needle, I suspect."

I stand, silent. It's not very often that people shock me.

I put my hand on his shoulder. "Mate, I'm giving you an opportunity here. I want you to take it, to make a successful life for yourself. You can do this. I know you can."

He doesn't answer.

Adrian tries desperately to change the subject. "Lets get your clothes ready for tomorrow." He claps his hands together in the gayest mannerism I have seen from him to date.

I smile broadly and shake my head. "You are so fucking gay, Murph."

Jarvis eyes widen to me in question. "Is he gay?"

"Total cocksucker." I smirk.

For the first time today I see a trace of a smile cross Jarvis' lips.

Adrian shrugs happily and starts pulling the clothing from the bags, spreading them out on the lounge. He puts the suits with the shirts, then lays out the belts and ties to wear with each outfit. "So, tomorrow, for work, wear this suit here." He gestures to it. "And this shirt, these shoes and this tie." He puts his hand on his chin in thought. "Did we get enough socks?"

Jarvis' face drops and he fiddles with his hands nervously.

I frown. "What's wrong?"

"I don't know how to do a tie," he whispers softly.

I swear, I can feel Adrian's heart melt across the floor.

Adrian and my eyes meet. "That's ok." He smiles gently.

Adrian and I immediately get the ties out of the bags and start tying them around our necks. We loosen them enough to get them off and lay them out for him. I look at my watch. Shit, I've got to go.

"I..." I hesitate, not wanting to leave this kid alone. "I have to go.

I'm picking up my wife and we are moving into our new apartment tonight."

Jarvis nods.

Murph's eyes glance between Jarvis and me. "You know what? I think I'm going to hang around here with Jarvis for a while and make him some dinner."

I smile at my wife. She's been to Hell and back, yet here she stands, looking up at me with love in her eyes.

"Are you ready to go to our new home, Mrs. Stanton?"

She smiles as she wraps her arms around me. "I am, my beautiful Lamborghini."

The apartment was ready to move into two weeks ago, but Natasha insisted on finishing her diary entries while we were at the hotel. She said she didn't want to go back there once we begin to move forward.

She has cried for the last two weeks, recounting the painful memories, but, hopefully, tonight will be a new start for us.

The apartment I have found is small – tiny, actually – but luxurious and cosy, which were Natasha's only prerequisites. She didn't want any part of finding the apartment, saying she trusted me to hold our future in my hands. Fifteen minutes later, we arrive, and I lead her by the hand up to our floor.

I have specifically asked that no security are with us when we enter. I want some time alone.

We approach the door and I bend down and pick her up like a bride in a rush. She giggles loudly.

"Are you carrying me over the threshold?"

"I am."

"I love you," she whispers as she kisses me gently.

"I love you, too." I smile into her lips.

I frown as I feel the tectonic plates of our world move into place. Maybe sometimes you have to experience dark to appreciate the light. Maybe I was meant to go to Prison to meet Jarvis. Maybe... no, positively, I am going to spend each day of the rest of my life adoring the woman I love and being the person she makes me.

I hand the key over to her. Natasha tries to open the door and we struggle and laugh as I bend to hold her at doorknob height.

When we open the door, Natasha's attention flies around and she gasps.

"Joshua," she whispers.

Thank fuck Cameron did his job.

I gently place her down with another kiss, her lips lingering on mine. "I fucking love you." She giggles as she puts both of her hands over her mouth in shock before she looks around.

The apartment is adorned with fresh flowers and the air is filled with their scent.

"Oh, Joshua," she cries. "Flowers, so many flowers."

I smile and drag her through the apartment by the hand. I do love this place. There are two small bedrooms on the lower floor, but I have turned one into an office, and the other one is for Didge when she wants to stay. The kitchen is small and timber with a little round table for two that sits in the corner. The apartment is decorated with antiques, lined with dark wooden floors, all of which are decorated with large, rich coloured rugs. Natasha walks around in awe wearing a huge smile on her face. "It is perfect. Absolutely perfect," she gasps.

"Like me?" I smirk. I did good finding this place.

Natasha smiles broadly. "Yes, like you." She kisses me, her tongue sweeping slowly through my mouth.

Natasha's eyes drift to the staircase, which sits to the left of the kitchen.

"What's up there?" she asks as she starts to drag me up the steps.

"Oh my God," she whispers when we get to the top.

It's the main bedroom, a loft above the living area. No less than two hundred candles flicker.

Natasha tears up and looks to me.

"I never gave you a wedding night," I whisper.

She frowns as she looks around once more. "Yes, you did."

I shake my head as emotion fills me. "No, we fucked on our wedding night." I take her lips in mine. "Tonight, we make love."

She smiles softly.

Oh. I nearly forgot! I go to the wardrobe and retrieve the small package wrapped in white paper and a gold bow, handing it over.

"What's this?" she asks.

"My wedding present."

She kisses me tenderly. "You are my present," she whispers.

"Open it."

Natasha slowly opens it and gasps when she sees the large diamond pendant on a thin gold chain. "Joshua." Her eyes are wide, almost questioning.

I smile and kiss her as I grab her around the waist roughly.

"Say thank you, wench."

She laughs into my kiss. "Thank you, wench," she repeats.

My lips drop to her neck. The sound of her laugh, the smell of her skin and the feel of her love makes forever seem too short.

And as her lips melt against mine, her hands pull my jacket off my shoulders.

"Naked. Now. I need you naked right now." She growls.

I happily oblige, I remove my jacket and shirt as she undoes my pants in desperation. She instantly drops to her knees and puts my dick in her mouth.

I close my eyes and hiss in appreciation. Her dark eyes watch me as she takes me deeply, in and out. I watch my cock slide from her mouth. This is supposed to be lovemaking but watching her do that just makes me want to rip her apart. My eyes find the hundreds of candles alight in the room.

Get it together, Stanton. Romantic... she deserves a romantic wedding night.

I pull her up to her feet and slowly take her clothes off as my lips stay locked with hers.

My neck gets tight and I crack it to release the tension.

"Oh, God, Josh, I fucking love that." She growls as she starts to climb me, wrapping her hands around my neck.

I smile as I lay her down on the bed. "I fucking love you," I whisper.

We kiss, and the feeling behind it has my eyes closing by their selves. My fingers find their home between her legs and I slide one in.

Oh, fuck, yeah. Burning hot and slick, just for me. I add another and slowly start to pump her with my fingers. Her body clings to me as I pull them out. This beautiful cunt is going to feel so fucking good around me tonight. I feel my pre-ejaculation rush to my head and start to drip.

My cock is hungry... so fucking hungry, and only one thing can feed my appetite.

She whimpers and arches her back off the bed. "Presh, do not start arching off the bed or I will lose control," I whisper in a pained voice.

She kisses me deeper as she arches again and I have to physically stop myself from dragging her beneath me. My cock is thumping, weeping and so damn hard, it's near painful.

Get it together, Stanton, I remind myself. Lovemaking... love... making. Not fucking. I shake my head and pull my fingers out. If I keep doing that, keep feeling the burning hot flesh inside my girl's body, it's all over.

She kisses me again and arches off the bed. "Josh, I need you to fill me."

I inhale deeply as I try to control myself.

Bloody hell, how do men do this gentle thing?

I need her around me again, so I push three fingers in and we both groan as her body contracts around me.

"Fuck me with those fingers," she whimpers. "Fuck me *hard*."

My breath quickens and my cock starts to take control of my actions. I rip her leg up aggressively and her eyes flash with arousal.

"You want to be finger fucked?" I hold my wet fingers up in front of her.

She nods as her dark eyes hold mine. She grabs my hand and puts my wet fingers in her mouth, sucking them dry. "I want to be finger fucked, then I want to be cock fucked, and then I want to be ass fucked," she purrs.

That's it. Control lost. I hold her legs back, pushing three fingers in, forcing her to clench around me. I pound her, my strong fingers surging in and out of her body until the bed slams against the wall.

"Joshua," she whimpers again as she lays back and shudders, her orgasm ripping through her.

When Natasha orgasms, I can't hold back. Her muscles contract so tightly around my fingers that I need to get my cock in there to feel it. I lose all control and any rational thought. I pull her legs over my shoulders and slam into her, she cries out. The muscles deep inside her quiver around me. I place her legs over my shoulders so I can hit the end of her, and I start to fuck her at piston pace. This is my favourite position by far. She can't move. I have her pinned to the bed and she can only lie there and take what I give her... what my cock decides to give to her. The only problem I have, is lasting. She feels so fucking good every time, I have to try and stop myself from coming.

It's always too quick. I part my legs wide on the mattress and start to ride my girl hard until she jerks, her second orgasm lifts her from the mattress and into my arms.

I sit back and splay her over me, spreading her legs wide. I hold her hips tight and piston up into my very own version of Heaven. She's swollen, dripping wet, and fucking perfect.

I need to be deeper, so I pull her hipbones back and forth over my cock, my eyes closing as I feel my ejaculation rip through all of my senses.

And then she kisses me and I smile into her beautiful lips as I try to catch my breath. We are both wet with perspiration and I glance around at the beautiful romantic candlelight we are basking in.

"I was trying to be romantic," I murmur into her neck.

She smiles and kisses me slowly, her tongue diving deeply into my mouth.

"Forget romantic," she replies. "You still have an ass to fuck."

I smirk. "God, my wife is a beautiful slut." I growl as I flip her onto the mattress and she laughs out loud. "You're about to fucking cop it."

CHAPTER 7

Six months later

TIME GOES FAST, but then it also stands so still. Joshua and I are back in L.A. We have recovered, to an extent. We're socializing again and we even have a party tonight at Carson's house, although the fucker still annoys me. Thankfully, Adrian and Bridge are also going, so they will keep me sane. Joshua is coping but angrier than he has ever been, kicking someone's ass every morning for sport. I once hated him fighting, but I now know that this is his therapy, this is his coping mechanism, and I need to let him fulfil that. He's filed lawsuits of defamation against most major tabloids over his court case. He refuses to let go of all the hurtful stories they sold and the lies that made them money. I don't blame him. On advice, suing them was the only way he can ensure that they don't keep hounding us, that they back off and let us live our lives in peace. We have suffered enough and he is putting a loud and clear message out that he has the money to fight, and he is prepared to spend every last penny to ensure our privacy. Two magazine editors have already lost their jobs, but he wants more blood. He has four more names on his hit list and I don't pity any of them one tiny bit. He's an angry man on a mission.

It's 2pm on a Friday, and I am at home alone. Bridget now works for Joshua three days a week, organising the company's work conferences, and Joshua works from home when he can, I'm not ready to go back to work. To be honest, I don't know if I ever will be ready? How can I be stable enough to look after someone else's mental health when I still struggle with my own? I have started to study online and, oh, I'm having a dabble at writing a book. It's totally shit, but I have the time, so why not try? It's a historical romance. Joshua is reading it by the chapter, and I write when we go to bed at night. He keeps telling me that he's going to have to lift his game if this is what guys in romance books do.

To be honest, I'm enjoying this time alone. I go to the gym... yes, you heard me right, I am going to the gym. Then I come home and study or write and potter around. We are looking for a new house to buy in Brentwood. Our apartment is gorgeous but Joshua misses his yard and pool. He wants a gym at home, and I wouldn't mind a decorating project, or should I say, I wouldn't mind a task to tackle with Adrian. My days are flying and I don't feel lonely at all like I thought I would.

I try to concentrate as I look at my computer screen but my eyes keep wandering to the brown paper bag on my desk.

A pregnancy test. I bought it at the pharmacy this morning with Max.

I was going to take it tonight when Joshua got home, but I think I want to do it now. No, I should wait for him.

I go back to my writing but my eyes wander by themselves again to the brown bag.

For fifteen minutes I continue to torture myself until I can't take it anymore. "Oh, fuck it." I snatch the bag and rip it open. I narrow my eyes as I carefully read the instructions. I have never done one before. I haven't taken the pill since I got back, but every month, like clockwork, my period has arrived. It's a conversation that Joshua and I haven't had. I know he doesn't want me to feel pressured and is purposely not bringing it up. I just want to surprise him.

Ok, so I just pee on the stick and one line is negative and two lines is positive. Hmm, sounds easy enough.

I go to the bathroom and do my thing on the stick. Then I sit on the kitchen bench and I watch it. I tap my fingers on the bench as I wait. My eyes flick to the clock. It's meant to take a few minutes, I suppose.

After the longest wait in history, there is only one line. What an anti climax. The front door opens. "Hi, Presh," Joshua's voice calls out through the apartment. Shit, I toss the test stick into the second drawer and slam it shut. I will deal with that later.

Joshua smiles as he comes around the corner and embraces me in his large arms. "Hello, my beautiful girl."

I smile against his lips. "Hello, my Lamborghini."

He kisses me gently. "How was your day?" he asks.

"It was good. How was yours?"

He shrugs. "Work was work."

He yawns as he goes to the fridge in search of a drink.

"Do we have to go tonight?" he asks.

"Yes."

"Mmm." He grumbles as he flicks the jug on and holds up a teabag.

I nod and smile. We don't even have to talk when tea is involved.

"I suppose I had better work out what to wear," I mutter to myself.

"Naked works for me."

I smirk. "You always want me naked."

He turns and cups my behind, pulling me to him aggressively as his tongue swipes slowly through my lips. "And you always comply," he whispers.

I giggle into my Margarita glass like a fool. Bridget and I are well on our way to drunk heaven at Carson's party, and we are finding everything and everyone hilarious. We're standing to the left of the pool, near the cocktail bar, and Adrian and Joshua are just behind us, talking. The music is loud and pumping inside where the people are dancing.

I feel two hands slip around my hips. "Keep dancing like that and you are going to cop it," he whispers in my ear.

I wiggle my hips in an exaggerated move.

"Bring it." I smirk into the side of his face.

Ben and Bridget are on amicable terms, and by amicable, I mean not talking. He doesn't come out with us anymore, which tells me that he still has feelings for her. She pretends that she doesn't care but I know she does. He has gone to South Africa for a holiday. Adrian's phone beeps a text in my hand and Bridget and I scream way too loudly. He smirks and takes it from us. At parties, in recent times, someone has been sending Adrian mysterious texts. The person doesn't tell him who it is, just how beautiful he looks and how badly they want to fuck him. This is a mystery that is getting solved tonight. I have been holding his phone for an hour as we wait.

He reads it out:

Adrian you look as beautiful as ever.

I narrow my eyes as I think of a reply. "Write this. As do you, I am watching you."

Bridget and I clink glasses.

"Excellent." Bridget nods. "Then he will think we know who it is."

Adrian and Joshua frown at each other. "That's a shit reply." Joshua shakes his head in disgust.

Bridget points at Adrian. "I know. Just write, I'm here, come and get it."

Adrian hands over the phone to us. "You two reply for me. I'm not in the mood for this stupid game of *Cluedo*."

I take the phone from him, and Bridget and I try to think of a witty comeback.

"It's a woman," says Joshua. "Any money it's a woman. A guy couldn't be fucked with this shit."

Adrian frowns. "Disappointing if it is."

Bridget puts her hand on her hip in disgust. "You should be so lucky to have sex with our species."

Adrian wraps his big arms around Bridget and squeezes her tight. "If you say so, Didge."

She smiles at his over the top affection. Didge and Adrian have become inseparable. They live together, they party together and they are getting over broken hearts together. Adrian went on a date just this week.

Hand the phone back to Adrian.

Another text comes through and we squeal in delight and look around. It is someone here. My eyes scan the crowd but I can't see anyone suspicious. It beeps again. I hand the phone back over to Adrian.

God, Adrian. I just want to fuck you so hard.

Adrian's eyes bulge and he laughs as he reads it out.

"It's a guy." I point my glass at him. "Girls don't say they are going to fuck you so hard."

Bridget nods. "Good point."

Joshua winces as he obviously gets a visual of Adrian copping it.

Adrian smiles mischievously and texts as he reads it out.

You must have me mistaken for someone else. I'm a virgin and am waiting for marriage.

Joshua rolls his eyes. "Witty," he replies flatly. We all laugh at his stupid comeback.

Serial party pest, the girl with the dark hair and big boobs, comes walking over.

"God, I fucking hate this bitch," Bridget mutters under her breath.

I drop my head to hide my smirk.

"Where is Ben?" she asks.

Bridget's back straightens in disgust. "He's at home with his wife," she replies coldly. I smirk. Didge is dying to piss her off. Lets see if she takes the bait.

The girl turns up her nose. "Idiot," she murmurs.

Bridget's temper starts to fray. "She is the one with a ring on his finger. I think that makes you the idiot."

I smile into my drink. Oh no, Didge has that bitchy tone in her voice. Cat fight impending.

The stupid girl shrugs. "Its not his ring finger I'm interested in."

I can practically see the red steam shoot from Bridget's ears. We are interrupted as everyone bursts into laughter and the crowd dissipate to allow someone through. My face drops in horror and I burst out laughing. Cameron and eight friends have just come straight from a buck's party. They are wearing hot pink t-shirts that say:

Yes

I fuck

On first

Dates

Along with Sombrero hats and bright pink lipstick. They are really drunk, I mean really drunk, with one man at the back having trouble standing.

"What have me and Ben got to do with you anyway." The girl snaps at Bridget.

Bridget leans in closer to the girl and I look over to Adrian, screwing up my face, all too aware that this is going downhill real quick.

"Ben is taken. Whore bag." Bridget sneers.

The stupid girl laughs as Cameron stumbles over and grabs me in an embrace. "Presh is here," he calls as he spins me around.

"Put her down!" Joshua snaps.

"Ben doesn't want to be taken, you stupid bitch," she sneers.

"What's going on?" Cameron slurs.

"I was just telling stupid here all about Ben's wife," Bridget replies.

Cameron pulls his head back in surprise. "Ben's married?" he slurs and questions.

Adrian and I get the giggles, while Joshua drags his hand down his face.

Adrian's phone beeps a text.

I'm coming to get you. Now.

His eyes widen and I snatch the phone from him.

A tall man comes over and stands next to us. Mine and Adrian's eyes meet in horror. This is him? This is the sexy texter? Oh my God, he looks like 'Weird Al' Yankovic.

Adrian drops his head to hide his smile.

"Adrian, I've come to take you home," he says in a Russian accent.

My mouth literally drops open, and this time it's Joshua who starts to chuckle.

"I'm warning you, pretty girl. I eat girls like you for breakfast," the girl snaps at Bridget.

Cameron interjects, "Excellent." He points his beer at her. "Bi-girls who get in my bed are my favourite kind of people."

"Fuck off, Cameron!" Bridget snaps.

"But... but she just said she's going to eat you for breakfast," he stammers, confused. Holy shit, he's so drunk.

"She's *not* eating me for breakfast," Bridget hits back.

Cameron exaggerates a nod. "Yeah, good, someone else." He frowns as he stumbles back. "Who's eating who for breakfast then?"

"I'm eating Adrian for supper," 'Weird Al' Yankovic announces.

Our eyes all turn to him in horror. What the hell? I put my hand over my mouth and burst out laughing.

"That is not happening," Adrian cries in an outrage.

"You can eat me then," he offers.

Adrian screws up his face in horror. "What?"

Oh God, this is hilarious. Joshua and I can hardly control the laughter we want to scream in this freak's face.

"You are lucky I don't drown you in the pool," Bridget tells Ben's friend.

The big-boobed bitch smiles as her eyes find the pool. "Wouldn't be the first time I have been in this pool," she purrs.

Bridget narrows her eyes as she loses control of her temper. "What the fuck is that supposed to mean?" she yells.

Oh shit. She is insinuating that has had sex with Ben in this pool. This is about to turn ugly.

"Go away, Avril!" Joshua snaps. Max comes over and stands to the right of us, obviously sensing the impending catfight.

"Avril Lavigne," Cameron repeats in a stupid voice as he raises his eyebrows in question.

"Cameron. Shut the fuck up!" Bridget yells.

I giggle. God, he's ridiculous when he's drunk. How does Avril Lavigne even come into this conversation?

"Come on, Adrian. Pleasure awaits you," 'Weird Al' purrs.

I bite my bottom lip to hold back my smile. This is like watching bad reality television.

Adrian puts his hands on his head in frustration. "Oh my God. Please... go away."

"I'm not going anywhere without you, Adrian."

"Oh man, just fuck off," Joshua barks at 'Weird Al' in frustration.

This night is going from hero to zero at a rapid rate.

"Are you saying that you had sex with Ben in this pool?" Bridget growls.

"I've had sex with Ben in most places."

"That's it…" Bridget snaps and throws her drink all over Avril Lavigne.

"You fucking bitch!" She screams as she dives for Bridget. Joshua steps in front of Bridget, while Avril makes an attempt to get around him and Max. Cameron staggers back as he is pushed out of the way, falling into a pot plant. He lands on the floor and his glass of beer smashes, spraying mine and Bridget's legs.

"Oww, Cameron!" Bridget and I yell as we look down at our legs in disgust. Avril Lavigne comes flying back at us, but Bridget gives her one almighty shove and she goes flying into the pool.

"Get in the car." Max sighs. The other guards appear and point to the car.

"Good one, Didge. Now we have to go home." I sigh, dejected. "I was having fun."

"Shut up. She fucking started it."

Adrian puts his arm around me from behind as we walk toward the front door. "Excellent timing, Bridget. That freak was stalking my ass."

I smile and turn to see what Joshua is doing only to see him pushing Cameron after us."

"I'm not fucking going home," Cameron protests.

"Get in the car. You are too drunk to leave here," Joshua tells him.

"Bridget is ruining our lives," Cameron snarls.

Avril Lavigne starts to yell at us as she climbs out of the pool. Bridget flips her the bird above her head as she walks in the opposite direction. We get out to the front yard and all climb into the large black SUV.

We sit still for a moment as we take in the last ten minutes and wait for our driver.

"Well, that night ended nicely, didn't it?." I sigh as the car begins to spin. It's a good thing, actually. I'm feeling very drunk and I know Joshua was about five seconds away from losing his shit with that girl. His temper knows no bounds these days.

"Yeah, well, I'm going to annihilate that bitch next time I see her." Bridget tough talks as she punches her fist.

"You should have ripped her top off," Cameron slurs. "That is the kind of shit I want to watch. Topless booby cat fighting"

"Oh my God." Adrian sighs, disgusted, and I smile broadly at my friend's stupid shenanigans.

Joshua winks at me and starts to shower my hand with kisses before he sucks on my index finger. He has that come fuck me look in his eyes, and I feel a flutter of arousal hit me.

"Pound Town," he mouths in the darkness of the car.

"I need a *Big Mac*, Stanton." I smirk as I eye him sitting next to me.

He puts his hand on his crotch and grabs it seductively. "I got one right here for you, baby."

From the seat behind us, we hear Adrian groan. "Oh, shit, this just gets worse."

From my bed, I hear the front door open downstairs, the car keys hit the foyer table with force, then I listen as he takes the stairs two at a time. I feel a rush of excitement sweep through me.

My man is home.

Once upon a time, he trained to fight. Now his fight is daily. Mentally battling his demons and physically fighting competitors at 6:00 a.m. every morning, I feel sorry for the poor bastards he fights. They don't stand a chance. He's changed. He's darker, damaged and unwilling to conform. Joshua Stanton is dealing with the last six months the best that he can… as am I.

We have each other, we get it, nobody else can understand the language we speak or the pain we have been through. I lie still, trying to recover from our night, and yet he has been up and to the gym. I know why he does it; he's trying to control the anger at what we have been through. He's still furious, furious at himself for letting it happen, furious at Amelie for doing what she did, and furious at the press for feeding on our nightmare. He turns the corner into our room and his dark eyes drop to my naked body on the bed. He's wet with perspiration and there's a tangible force, a feeling of adrenaline pumping through his body out onto me where I lie. His t-shirt comes off slowly over his head, and he drops his pants to reveal that beautiful rock hard body.

"How was your fight?" I whisper as my eyes lower to my name on his side.

He smiles sexily as he walks around the side of the bed, surveying me. He doesn't answer as his hand drops to between his legs and he gives himself three slow hard strokes. My breath catches. He hasn't said a word or touched me and yet, as always, just the sight of him makes me good to go. "You look exceptional, Mrs. Stanton," he whispers as his hand continues to stroke his cock.

I hold my breath and open my legs just that little bit farther. Joshua cracks his neck hard as his dark eyes stay fixed between my legs.

His tongue slides over his bottom lip before he drops his head and begins to lick my inner thigh.

"Give me my breakfast. I'm fucking starving."

I lay back and close my eyes. Mr. Stanton is here, like he is most mornings when he returns from fighting. The adrenaline in his system is through the roof and I'm the lucky girl he releases it on. Our sex is rougher and less controlled than it has ever been, but it's also never been so hot. I'm putty in his dominant hands.

I crave his control over my body. I crave the way he takes what he needs without a care in the world.

His strong hands hold my legs apart and his hot tongue swipes through my flesh.

"Hmm," he groans into me.

My hands fall to the back of his head.

"Oh, you fucking taste good, my beautiful girl," he whispers.

I shudder immediately and close my eyes. If I watch him do that, I will come in five seconds flat.

He starts to really eat me, dragging my body up and down his face. His sharp whiskers are grinding but it's a pleasurable burn, a pain I have become accustomed to, the pain is my addiction. His tongue swirls around and around and I feel myself buckle beneath him.

"Still," he orders as he rips my legs back to the bed. "Give me what I need." He growls.

"What do you need?" I whisper.

"A creamy orgasm on my tongue," he whispers as his eyes hold mine. He gently bites my clitoris and stretches it back from my body. I jump in pain and then he circles it gently again with his tongue. This is what he does so well, shifting tempo. The hard bites followed by the gentle licks, the strong hands holding my legs down to the bed versus the gentle kisses on my inner thigh. The look he gives, telling me that he is about to rip me apart, and then the tender kisses that show me he loves me.

I love this man. I love all of this man. The dark, the fucked up, the sex craved maniac.

He pushes three fingers into me aggressively and I flinch off the mattress at the burn.

"I need some pain this morning, baby. Can you give me that?" His dark eyes watch me as I struggle to accept his large fingers.

I nod. "Give it to me," I whisper.

He pushes me hard again and I sigh in pleasure. He sits up and starts to ride me hard with his hand, so much so that the bed starts to hit the wall with force. *Thump, thump, thump,* the heavy sound of the bed hitting the wall matches my oncoming orgasm. My legs start to close and I quiver as I lose all coherent thought. He bends and starts to tongue my clitoris gently as his fingers pound into me aggressively. The combination pushes me over. My body lurches forward, the force of the strong orgasm taking over, and before I know what's happening, Joshua has my legs over my shoulders and he's pushing into me hard.

He stays still for a moment, letting me adjust to his brutal length. No matter how much he is aroused, he always pauses after he has pushed in to allow me to adjust to his size. Joshua knows he is a large man and he sees it as his responsibility to make sure he doesn't hurt me. But, fuck, I love it when he does.

He holds himself up on tensed arms as he waits for my permission.

"Go," I whisper. "Fuck me."

His eyes close in reverence and he slides out slowly. My calves are next to his face and he kisses the inner ankle of one foot tenderly.

This feels so fucking good. He spreads his knees widen to gain control and pushes forward again.

"That beautiful, sweet cunt of yours feels so fucking good around my cock."

I clench hard and he bends to kiss me aggressively.

I smile, a proud of myself smile, and he bites my bottom lip.

I watch the sheen of perspiration that covers my beautiful creature as he holds my ankles wide in the air, feeding his desires with my body. "You're so fucking wet. Dripping for me," he purrs as he watches his cock disappear into me. Our bodies start to make a loud slapping sound as he fucks me hard.

Bloody hell, once again, I start to quiver. Stop dirty talking; you know it's my undoing.

The sight of his sweaty, muscular body, the sound of my wet skin clinging to his, and the feeling of his thick, engorged cock sliding through me is too much.

"Joshua," I whimper.

He picks me up and throws me over onto my knees, yanking my legs apart as far as they go. Then he is riding me hard while he grips both of my hips and slams me back onto his cock. He goes harder and faster, until he's pushing my shoulders down onto the mattress to get deeper.

This is how he fucks me. He's never deep enough, never hard enough, never close enough.

"You feel so fucking good." He growls and stills, and I feel his cock jerk deep inside of me, forcing me to close my eyes as another orgasm steals my ability to articulate anything. I struggle for breath as my heart hammers in my chest.

And then, as if by some miracle, my gentle man comes back to me and showers the curve of my spine with tender kisses. He lays his body over mine and I feel his lips on my cheek before he nibbles my ear.

"I love you," he whispers.

I smile breathlessly. "I love you."

I feel him smile broadly. "I love fucking you more."

We fall onto the bed in a tangled mess and kiss, long slow kisses. Even when we have rough sex, there is an overwhelming feeling of love between us, an overwhelming feeling of what we have is so very precious. And we can never forget that because it governs most of our daily thoughts.

We lie still for ten minutes before Joshua stands and kisses my hip.

"Shower." He slaps my behind.

"Hmm." I'm dozing.

"Come on. Up. It's eleven. I'm making breakfast."

I drift off but vaguely hear him shower, go downstairs and fuss around in the kitchen.

I feel the bed bounce as Joshua jumps on it. "What's this?" he demands.

Hmm, I keep my eyes closed and pull the blankets over my head. God, stop being so fucking perky. I'm feeling very hungover here.

"Natasha."

"Hmm." I pull the blankets back over my head in a fuck off not now symbol.

"I know what this is."

"Oh God, Joshua, I want to sleep in," I groan.

"So, you are taking pregnancy tests without me now?"

Huh? My eyes open instantly. Oh fuck. I left it in the drawer. I pull the blankets even farther over my head.

"I did it the other day." I close my eyes again; God, I am really tired here.

"Why didn't you tell me?"

"Because I was only going to tell you if it was positive."

"Why?"

"I wanted to surprise you."

"Oh." He thinks for a moment. "So, it was negative then?"

"Yes."

He starts to tap me on the head with it to annoy me. "One egg or two?"

I snatch it from him. "Stop it."

"Do you want avocado?"

"Yes, please." I roll over onto my back and hold up the test to look at it, I frown.

"What?"

I frown as I try to wake up. Am I seeing things here?

"What are you frowning at?" he asks.

"Why are there two lines on this test?"

136

He takes it from me. "What do you mean?"

"I mean, why are there two lines on this test?"

He shrugs as he looks at it. "I don't know, you tell me. You took the test."

I keep staring at it in horror. I got totally drunk last night.

"What do two lines mean?" he asks.

"Two lines means positive," I whisper.

"It does?"

I put my hand over my mouth as I try to think. "It was one line the other day."

He stands, and then sits back down, and then he stands again.

I shake my head. "It must be dodgy. Maybe they don't age right."

Joshua frowns at me. "Do we have another test?"

"Um." I think for a moment. "Downstairs in a brown paper bag in my hand bag, under my desk in the office."

Joshua jumps up and practically runs down stairs. I sit up in bed. Fuck. Why did I drink so much last night?

He returns as he rips open the bag and fumbles around getting the second test out of the bag.

He passes it over and smiles cheekily.

My eyes hold his and I snatch it from him. "It's negative, don't give me that hopeful look. You are going to be disappointed. See, this is why I didn't tell you. I don't want to disappoint you."

He kisses me gently. "You could never disappoint me."

"W-we are not ready to be parents," I stammer.

"Why not?"

"I got hopelessly drunk last night. You are suing people and all the aunties and uncles are totally out of fucking control. Bridget is cat fighting and Cameron's a Dr. Deviant. Adrian's attracting weirdos." I throw my hands in the air in defeat. "Who was I kidding? No way can I be a parent."

"We are all normal," he whispers against my lips.

"We are crazy," I murmur in a panic.

He kisses me gently. "I love our crazy." His lips linger on mine. "I need our crazy."

I melt a little and walk to our bathroom. Joshua follows me.

"Wait outside," I tell him quietly. God, he's not watching me pee on a stick. No way in Hell. It's humiliating enough to have to watch myself.

He frowns and nods. "Fine."

I pee on my stick and then walk out and find him reading the instructions with intense concentration.

"Here." I hand it to him.

He bites his lip as he tries to contain his smile, taking it from me. He begins to watch it as I pace at the end of the bed and shake my hands.

My heartbeat is racing and my eyes keep looking up to find him. For the longest five minutes in history he sits still, focused on our stick.

I watch in slow motion a huge smile spreads across his face.

I frown. "What?" I whisper almost afraid of the answer. "What does it say?"

He stands and then bends and kisses me. "Baby Stanton is in the house."

My eyes widen.

Dear, God.

CHAPTER 8

Joshua.

I SMILE AS I stand in the elevator on my way up to my office. In fact, I have been smiling since Saturday morning at eleven o'clock. Even when I try to wipe the smile from my face, it just won't go. I am completely consumed with emotion and never have I been so fucking in love with my girl.

Natasha doesn't want to tell anyone until she's at twelve weeks. Apparently that's standard practice.

How do you keep a secret like this? It's impossible.

The doors open and I exit into the corridor.

"Girls." I smile as I walk past reception.

"Hello, Mr. Stanton," they all call as their eyes linger on me.

I walk straight into Adrian's office. He's on the phone, facing the window, but he spins in his chair to look at me as I enter.

I smile broadly and he frowns in question.

"Who's that?" I mouth.

He shakes his head and rolls his eyes. "Yes, I understand your point of view and I will take it up with Human Resources."

I smirk. A disgruntled employee, no doubt.

He listens again and raises his eyes to the ceiling in frustration.

I sit on his desk and buzz Tiffany. "Tiffany, could you please bring in Adrian's and my coffee, plus a cappuccino, to his office, please?"

"Yes, sir," her polite voice answers.

I twirl my finger in the air to signal for him to hurry it up.

He frowns again and shakes his head as he listens.

"Get off the phone," I mouth.

"I'm fucking trying," he mouths back.

My phone beeps a text. It's Cameron.

Where are you?

I text back.

In Murph's office.

Two minutes later, Cameron walks into Adrian's office, followed by Tiffany with our coffees.

"Hey," he calls. "What's up? What couldn't wait?"

I gesture to Adrian. "Wait for him."

He takes a seat at the desk and yawns into his hand. "Thank God you made me go home on Friday night. I can hardly remember being at Carson's.

"God, you're an ugly chick." I wince.

"That lipstick is bloody hard to get off, you know. I had to work yesterday and my lips were fucking burning from scrubbing the shit off. I had to wear lip balm."

I smirk. "Get off the phone," I mouth at Adrian.

"Who is he speaking to?" Cameron frowns.

I shrug. "Some whiner."

Adrian finally hangs up and looks at me, deadpan, as he takes his coffee from the tray. "Why are you in my office?"

I smile an exaggerated smile.

They both look at me in confusion.

"Natasha's pregnant."

They both stare at me dumbfounded, not saying anything.

"Did you hear me?"

"What?" Adrian frowns.

"Serious?" Cameron asks.

"Deadly." I smile.

"Deadly pregnant?" I hear a touch of excitement fill Adrian's voice.

"I'm not supposed to tell anyone."

Cameron grabs me in a rough handshake and puts his head with mine.

"We don't count," Adrian whispers as he lets his excitement flow and grabs me in an embrace.

"I know. You both don't count. But don't let on I've told you, especially not to Natasha."

"Oh my God." Adrian starts to jump around and then his face falls as he joins the dots. "But... Tash was drunk on Friday night."

"Yes, she didn't know." My eyes flicker to Cameron. "Is that a problem?"

He screws up his face. "Not ideal. But a lot of women don't always know at first. It should be ok."

I smile brightly again. "That's what Dr. Google said. What else should I know?" I ask.

"About pregnancy?"

I nod as I sip my coffee.

His face falls. "Are you only telling me so you can get medical information?"

"Of course."

He curls up his top lip and shakes his head at Adrian. "Figures," he mumbles under his breath. "How far along is she?"

I shrug. "I don't know. We are going to the doctors this afternoon."

"We are having a baby?" Adrian repeats. "For reals."

"I'm having a baby." I grin. "You are just helping."

Adrian puts his hand over his heart. "Oh, I just want to squeeze my girl."

"She's my girl and *you* don't fucking know yet," I mutter into my coffee cup.

"Oh, right." He flops down onto the lounge. "We should go get drunk or something."

I smile and I look to Cameron who is smiling like an idiot. "We really should," he replies.

I shake my head. "No, we're going to the doctors later."

"Tonight?" he asks.

"No." I frown. "I'm not leaving her alone for one minute. I had to drag myself to work today."

Adrian lies back on the lounge and holds his heart. "My Cinderella is having a baby. This is the best news ever."

My attention returns to Cameron. "What about sex?"

"Sex is fine."

My eyes hold his in question.

He tilts his head to the side already knowing my question. "You mean rough sex?"

I nod subtly.

"How rough is rough?"

I lift my chin defiantly.

"Rough, rough. Like rough?" he questions.

I give him a lopsided smile and tilt my head to the side, not really answering him.

"I don't know much about the female anatomy, but I do know that you can't do that. Put a fucking cork in it, you sex maniac!" Adrian snaps as he runs his hands through his hair in disgust.

I roll my eyes.

Cameron thinks for a moment and shrugs. "I think its ok, but maybe just tone it down a bit."

"Oh." I frown. Shit, I gave it to her hard on Saturday morning. What if I have already done damage?

"You already did it, didn't you?"

"Perhaps," I murmur.

"And she's ok?"

I shrug. "She seems ok."

"Then it's ok."

I turn to Adrian and he shrugs. The office door opens and Jarvis wanders in. "Oh, hello." He smiles.

"Hi, mate."

"Hey," Cameron calls. "How are your arms?" Cameron smirks.

"Ripped off the fucking bone." He sighs as he starts to file things away in Adrian's drawers.

I smile broadly and throw the boys a wink. Cameron and Murph have taken Jarvis under their wing. They take him everywhere, even dragging him to their early morning gym sessions. He's acting like he hates it, but I know he loves the time they spend with him. Even Tash and Didge are enamoured with our young friend. I smile. I can't say I blame them. I'm quite taken with him myself.

"Ok, losers. I got to go to work." Cameron sighs as he stands. "Are you cooking me dinner, Murphy?" he asks.

Murph's eyes flick to Jarvis. "You want to come for dinner?"

"Sure," Jarvis replies casually.

Adrian's looks at me. "You guys want to come over for dinner, too?"

I shake my head. "No, thanks. I'm taking Tash out."

Adrian smiles a *we have a secret* smile and I shake my head. "I will be in my office if you need me."

I walk out down the hall and Tiffany calls me. "Mr. Stanton?"

"Yes?"

"Your appointment is in your office."

"Who is it?" I frown. "I haven't opened my diary yet."

"He made the appointment weeks ago. He's from the Australian Medical board."

"Why is he here?"

She shrugs. "I don't know. It's weird, actually. The appointment was made in one name and then when he turned up today he had a different name."

"What is his name?"

She walks back over to her desk and picks up her diary. "James Brennan."

I feel the floor move from beneath me and, as if working on autopilot, I storm toward my office, pulling the door open in a rush.

He stands with his back to me, staring out the window, wearing a dark grey suit and cream shirt. He slowly turns toward me.

"Hello, son."

I glare at him as shock starts to trickle into my bloodstream.

I feel like it's the first time I have ever seen his face. We look alike. We fucking look alike. He stands at my height, six feet four inches tall. His hair is greying at the temples and his skin is olive. But it's the eyes that are the mirrors. I drop my head and swallow the lump in my throat. How can I look like him?

"Get out before I fucking kill you," I whisper.

He stays still, his eyes hold mine.

'That's no way to talk to your father."

"You are not my father."

"Ah." He smiles sarcastically. "We both know that's not true now, don't we?"

I step toward him as I feel the adrenaline start to pump through me.

He raises his chin in defiance.

"So help me God," I whisper. "I will tear you apart, limb by limb."

He glares at me.

"Get out!"

"No. You will listen to what I have to say."

"The hell I will."

"I'm not here for myself. You are too Stanton to ever be my son."

'Thank fuck for that." I growl.

"I'm here for your mother."

"How dare you? I said get out."

"You haven't spoken to her in six months."

My hostile eyes hold his.

"And you have yourself to thank for that." I sneer.

"What did you want her to do? Pine her whole life for a husband who took his pleasure in other beds." I start to hear my heart beat in my ears. "Is that really all she deserved?"

"You were his best friend."

"And I saw how he treated her."

"Get out."

"He never loved her."

I can't even look at him and my eyes focus on one spot on the carpet.

"I love her, Joshua. I have always loved her."

"That's why you beat her?"

He pauses. "We..." He tries to articulate his thoughts. "It's true we have a volatile relationship. You don't know how many times I begged her to leave him – to come out to the world about our love."

"Liar."

"She loves me."

"If she loved you she would have gone with you."

"Would she?" He raises his eyebrows in question. "You and I both know there is only one reason she stayed."

I glare at him. "You blackmailed her for my money."

He shakes his head. "No. She loaned me the money to start up another business. It was a short term loan."

"Fuck off. You're lying. What about Wilson? I don't see you knocking on his door?"

"Wilson is next on my list," he tells me dryly. "But it's you that upsets her. Her beloved Joshua Stanton." He sneers. "She sacrificed a whole lifetime of happiness to live in a loveless marriage... for *you*. She didn't know about Wilson until recently."

"You have approximately ten seconds to get out of here or you will be leaving on a stretcher."

"You are more like me than you know." He smirks sarcastically and I frown. "It feels good to be violent doesn't it?"

Violence has long been my favourite hobby. Dear, God, I feel the pain of truth seep into my bone marrow.

"Some days, you just feel like you will explode if you don't get the anger out." He replies.

I drop my head. "No." I murmur to myself.

"Like the desire to hurt someone will eat you alive if you don't get it out."

"Shut up."

"How many times do you kick someone's ass in a week, Joshua?"

"Shut up!" I yell.

"Can you imagine being so in love with a woman that you can't see straight? To have a child with her and for her to deny it to the world? For the child to be bought up by another man?"

My heart starts to race.

"We were in each others arms every damn day, yet she went home to him every night. It killed me."

I stare at him.

"Do you blame me for losing control with her. Can you imagine if Natasha was married to someone else? If your child was brought up with another man's name when you knew that she loved you?"

My baby comes to my mind and my eyes mist over. "Get out," I whisper.

"Yes, we fought, but I loved her. With every ounce of my being, I loved her."

I can think of anything but my Natasha and our baby. I can't even imagine what he is telling me. Would I ever hit Natasha if I lost control? No. I could never.

"Talk to your mother, Joshua. She needs you."

Pain lances my heart. I need her, too.

I don't know what to say, I have no words. I look at him through blurry eyes. "Goodbye. It's been nice never knowing you."

His tortured eyes hold mine. "I wish I could say the same."

I turn and leave my office on, what I swear will be my last interaction with that man.

I upload the last of the files and blow out a deep breath. It's three o'clock and I have just wanted to go home since my earlier visit from James, but I haven't let myself. He's not getting to me. My door opens and Natasha's beautiful face comes into view.

"Hello." She smiles.

I stand immediately and walk over to her. "I thought I was picking you up at four?"

She wraps her arms around my neck and I push her hair behind her shoulders. "I wanted to check you were alright." Her lips meet mine.

I smile. "I'm fine."

"Were you shocked?"

"Yes."

"Did it go ok?"

I shake my head. "No." I inhale a breath in her hair. "But I didn't kill him so that's something."

She smiles as her tongue gently rims my lips. "Why do I have two extra guards today?"

My hand instinctively drops to her stomach. "Because there are two of you now."

She raises her eyebrows as she places her hand over mine. "Are you serious?"

"I am."

"Joshua, I have nine months to go. Are you going to be overbearing the whole time?"

I smile and kiss her gently. "You have seven months and three weeks left, and you have not even began to see overbearing yet, Presh."

I lead her over to my desk by the hand, drop into my chair and pull her down onto my lap. I inhale her scent deeply and smile. All in the world seems perfect again. We kiss, gently at first and then deeper and I feel my arousal start to rise. Every time, every damn time I think I can't feel closer to this beautiful woman, something happens to intensify our intimacy, taking it to another level.

I beam.

"What?" She smirks.

"I told you my boys were good swimmers."

She giggles. "You are such a confident bastard."

The door opens and Adrian walks in without noticing me. He stops mid-step when he sees me. "N-natasha," he stammers.

"Hi, baby." She smiles.

She stands to kiss him and he grabs her in an embrace, squeezing her. He stands back and holds her at arms length and smiles a swoony smile. He squeezes her again. "Oh, you look so beautiful today," he gushes.

She looks over at me, her face serious. "You told him."

"Way to go, Murph," I hiss.

He screws up his face. "But I'm so excited. I promise I won't tell anyone," he stammers.

"Did you tell Cameron, too?"

"Maybe." I wince.

She smirks. "It's ok. I told Didge, Mum and Abbie, too. I couldn't hold it in."

Adrian sighs with relief and bends to kiss her stomach. "Hello, in there, it's your favourite uncle. The good looking one." He hangs off her hips with a huge smile on his face.

I smirk and Natasha rolls her eyes. "This is going to be a long eight months." She sighs as she puts her hand on his head.

Natasha

I sit in the car as the scenery flashes by, my heart is beating through my chest. I reach over and grab Nicholas' hand and he squeezes it back in a reassuring gesture. I'm twelve weeks pregnant and about to do something that I know is going to cause Armageddon. Nicholas and I are going to the prison, four hours south of L.A. to visit the young boy who kept me alive when I was held hostage. I have too many questions, too many unanswered things that I need to tie up. I lost twenty-four hours of my life and I can't let it go no matter how hard I try. I need closure. I need to know what happened to me. Nicholas has been giving me phone therapy sessions from London, and he and I both think that this will give me some sort of closure. He has flown home from London for three days to come with me. Joshua doesn't know I'm going and I have lied to the guards, telling them we are picking up a stroller from a shop. There is one car in front of us and one behind. I'm more guarded than the fucking Queen these days. Max is driving and I know he is onto something. He keeps looking at me and raising an eyebrow in question. He knows I wouldn't drive four hours to buy a stroller with Nicholas in tow. I don't want to do this when I have a baby at home, and I don't want to go there when I'm noticeably pregnant, either. He could be transferred to another prison or given parole and I will never get my much-needed answers. I need to get this over with now so I can deal with it before the baby comes. Max is driving, so I can't even discuss with Nicholas what I am going to say. We are sitting here, both pretending that we are on a shopping trip. This Russian spy thing we have going on is only adding to my nerves.

"What is the address?" Max asks for the second time.

Nicholas' eyes meet mine. I can't tell him the address until we are nearly there. If he works out where we are going, he will ring Joshua. Shit, this is messed up.

"I have the address in my bag, just head into town and I will find it," I reply nervously.

"Ok." His eyes flash at me in the rear view mirror. He calls the car in front of us. "Get off at the next exit."

"Gotcha," the voice replies.

I grab the small notepad from my bag and give it to Nicholas who types the address into his Maps app to look it up.

"Actually, Max, while I am here, I want to quickly visit a work colleague." Nicholas replies casually.

Max's eyes flicker to me again in the mirror. "Where at?"

"We will go to his work."

"Where does he work?"

"Turn right up here," Nicholas instructs.

The car in front of us falls behind so we now have two cars trailing us. My heart really starts to hammer.

"Second left." Replies Nicholas.

I can see it. The large grass area of the prison and the fences. Fuck, am I really going to do this?

"Natasha, you can come in with me."

We get to the gates and Max narrows his eyes in thought.

"He works at the prison?"

"Yes, I'm just going to invite him out for lunch with us."

Max enters slowly and goes into the car park to park the car.

"I-I will come with you," I stammer as I open the door.

"No, you won't!" Max snaps. "You will wait here."

Panic hits me and I start to hotfoot it across the car park to the prison's front doors.

"Natasha?" Max yells. "Get back here."

"I'm going in. I need answers, Max."

His face falls as he puts the puzzle together. "No!" he yells.

The other guards all start to get out of their cars.

I make it to the front doors with Nicholas hot on my heels and turn to look out the window to see Max on the phone. Shit, he's ringing Joshua.

My heart is thumping so fast.

Nicholas walks to the reception. "We have an appointment to see an inmate."

My eyes turn to look back outside to see the guards all pacing. They aren't allowed to touch me and I know they won't physically drag me from here.

My phone rings and I jump. The name Lambo lights up the screen and I flick it to silent. Nicholas turns and looks at me, shaking his head.

Fuck. I run my hands through my hair.

The phone rings out but then rings again straight away.

A text beeps through.

ANSWER YOUR FUCKING PHONE!

Oh my God. He's going to kill me.

It rings again and I close my eyes as I answer. "Hello," I whisper.

"Where the fuck are you?" he shouts.

"I need answers."

"Where are you?" he screams.

"I'm at the prison. I'm visiting the boy who kept me alive."

"What?" He yells so loud, I have to hold the phone away from my ear.

"Get in the fucking car and get your ass back here right now. How dare you do this?"

My eyes tear up. It's been a long time since Joshua has been so angry with me. I forgot how scary he is.

"Don't you even think about going in," he growls. "I mean it! So help me God, Natasha."

I swallow my fear. "I love you." I hang up and turn my phone off. I will deal with him later.

The large door bolts open and Nicholas turns to me. "You ready?"

We walk down a long corridor and into a room. It reminds me of the room I used to see Jes in when we first met.

Nicholas takes a seat next to me and the young boy is led in. His eyes meet mine and he drops his head in shame before he sits down.

I sit and stare at him as he looks at the floor. Is he fucking kidding? He put me though Hell and doesn't even have the guts to look me in the eye.

Nicholas' phone rings and he switches it straight off. Shit, that was Joshua.

I sit still as my time locked in that room is replayed in my head. He doesn't look up and he doesn't acknowledge me.

What a fucking coward.

Fury starts to rise and I take a deep breath to calm myself down. Nicholas and I talked about me getting upset could endanger my baby. I need to stay calm and get my answers, then leave.

"Why?" I ask.

He looks down.

"I asked you a fucking question. Answer it."

"Why do you think?"

I glare at him. He's different to what he was in the house. Prison hasn't been kind to him. He's harder, colder.

"She offered me money, more than I could refuse."

"How long was it planned?"

He shrugs.

"Think!" I snap.

"Couple of months."

"Who drugged me?"

He sits back and rolls his eyes. "If you came here for an apology, I'm sorry." He sneers.

I sit forward as fury rips through me. "I didn't come to you for an apology, you conceited little prick. I came to find out how you got me off the boat."

His eyes hold mine.

"And the sooner you tell me the sooner I will leave. Who drugged me?"

"A waitress."

"Who was the waitress?"

"One of Amelie's friends. You nearly didn't drink it."

I frown as a cold shiver runs down my spine. There were people watching and waiting for me to drink fucking poison at that wedding.

I swallow my anger. "When I got back to the boat... what happened?"

He doesn't answer me.

"Answer the question." Nicholas growls.

"There were two scuba divers already under the boat when you arrived."

I frown.

"Carl and another man."

"Go on."

"As soon as the boat you arrived on drove off, they climbed aboard."

"Straight away?"

"They needed the sound of the engine to drown out them climbing into the boat."

Oh God. I put my head into my hands as fear runs through me.

"They were only on there for ten minutes when you were unconscious."

I stare at him through tears.

"He was only supposed to nick your vein, but the knife was too sharp."

A tear falls onto my cheek as I run my thumb over my deep scar. I can almost feel it cutting me again.

"There was too much blood. They had bandages to wrap it before they put you in the water."

I frown as I imagine men in scuba diving gear smearing my blood all over the deck and wrapping my arm in a bandage.

"You were off the boat within fifteen minutes of them climbing on it."

I frown. "I thought this happened in the still of the night?" God, the guards would have all been chatting only two hundred metres away.

He shakes his head. "It had to be done straight away or they would have been heard."

"They swam you back to shore and gave you oxygen from their tanks."

A wave of emotion starts to flood my senses as if memories are coming back to me.

"That's where I came into it."

I raise an eyebrow in question.

"I was in the back of a horse float by the water in the forest. They loaded you into the back of it and I looked after you while they drove us to the house."

"You stitched me in the back of a horse float?" I ask. Oh my God, I can't believe this shit.

"Yes. I couldn't stop the bleeding. I had to."

Nicholas grabs my hand for support.

"When we got to the house, I gave you a transfusion of my blood."

He saved my life. I stare at him for an extended time. "Thank you," I whisper through tears.

For the first time he looks remorseful.

I sit for a moment, not sure what to ask next. There are more things I should know but I just don't want to be here anymore. It was the getting me off the boat information that I so desperately needed. I don't want to hear any more of this vile horror. I look at him one last time and I stand.

"I'm ready to go. Goodbye."

"Goodbye, Natasha."

I walk out into the hall as if The Devil has been set free from my soul. I can finally breathe.

CHAPTER 9

IT'S JUST GONE dark when the car pulls into the underground parking lot of our apartment. There has been complete radio silence. Joshua hasn't called, so he obviously knows I've left the prison and am on my way home. As we drive around, I see him standing on the curb near the entrance to the elevator. There are two guards standing back and Ben is leaning up against Joshua's car. They're all waiting for me. How long has he been standing there? His hands are in his suit trouser pockets, and the look on his face is murderous. I feel my fear rise and perspiration starts to burn my armpits. I haven't seen him this angry since he found Jesten in my apartment that night.

"Fucking hell," Max mutters under his breath. "This is going to be good."

I blow out a breath and Nicholas grabs my hand reassuringly. Nicholas flies back to London tomorrow.

"Thank you for coming with me," I whisper. "I really appreciate you coming all this way to support me."

He smiles. "It had to be done. I'm glad you are feeling better."

Max parks the car and I get out slowly. Joshua stands still on the spot. Something he never does. He always walks to me and then walks me back. He's severely pissed. I walk toward him and his eyes don't leave my face.

"H-hello," I stammer.

He doesn't say anything.

Nicholas is the first to speak. "Joshua."

Joshua holds up his hand and cuts him off. "Don't fucking speak. Get in your car and fuck off before I knock you out."

My eyes widen. Holy crap, I'm dead meat.

Nicholas takes his cue and bends to kiss me. "Call me," he whispers awkwardly before taking off across the car park toward his car. Joshua turns and walks to the lift, pressing the button.

"Don't be rude to Nicholas," I stammer nervously as I follow him.

His head snaps around, but he holds his tongue and, after a deathly silence, he speaks. "I will do whatever the hell I fucking like."

We get into the lift with Max and Ben and stand silently. This is so awkward with them around. I think I want to run to Bridget's. Joshua's scaring even me. My eyes watch the dial as the floors shoot past. Shit, I don't want to get out of the lift. The door finally opens and Joshua holds his hand out. My eyes fall to Max and he nods. That's his *I will be out here if you need me* nod. I smile in thanks. Joshua opens the door and I walk in, The door closes and he throws the keys so hard at the wall that they put a hole in the plasterboard. I jump in fright and start to shake my head nervously. "Joshua, please understand…"

"Understand what?" he yells.

"I needed answers," I cry.

His eyes narrow. "I need a few fucking answers myself." He sneers.

I cringe at the venom in his voice. Oh God, I've never seen him like this.

"At what point, Natasha, did you think that going to a prison to see someone who tried to murder you…" His voice is cold and calm and I swallow my fear. "Was a good fucking idea?" he screams.

My tears fall.

157

He holds up a finger in my face. "Don't you dare! Don't you fucking dare start your water works bullshit."

I stand still, unsure what to say. My bottom lip is trembling. "Joshua, calm down," I whisper.

"Calm down?" he yells. "Calm down? I am married to a self-centred liar who put my baby's life at risk today."

My face falls. "This is the first time I have ever lied to you."

"I am way, way, beyond fucking calming down."

"The baby's life wasn't at risk," I try to tell him.

"Wasn't it?" he shouts.

"I knew what I was doing."

"Just like the night on the boat when you told Ben to go." He shakes his head as he gathers his thoughts. "You knew what you were doing that night too, didn't you? You didn't need protection that night, either, did you, Natasha?"

My eyes close. He had to bring that up, didn't he?

My tears fall and I shake my head. "No. I knew you wouldn't let me go."

"Because I'm trying to protect you!" he screams so loud that I jump back.

"You're scaring me," I whisper.

"You should be fucking scared."

My face falls. "Stop it," I breathe.

He stares at me for an extended time and then closes his eyes.

"I'm scaring myself," he replies coldly. He comes really close to my face. "You lied to me today. You betrayed me today." He growls.

I shake my head as my tears fall. "No, Joshua, I would never do that."

He turns away from me and punches the wall and it crumbles under his fist.

"Stop it," I cry.

He turns and his wild eyes hold mine as he struggles for control.

"Please understand," I whisper.

"Understand this. I can't be around you right now." He picks up his keys.

"Where are you going?" I whimper.

"Away from you."

"No. Joshua, don't go," I cry. "Where are you going?"

He turns and walks out of the apartment and slams the door. My face scrunches up, tears falling. Oh God. Now I've done it.

I fall onto my bed and wail.

"It's 2:00 a.m. and Bridget and I are on my lounge watching the clock. Joshua hasn't come home and I don't know where he is.

"Where the hell is he?" Bridget frowns. "I've had enough of his shit."

"He was so mad, Didge; I've never seen him so mad."

She rolls her eyes. "What were you thinking? Why didn't you just tell him?"

I shrug sadly. "I don't know. I knew he would be mad but I didn't expect this mad."

"How mad, like on a scale from one to ten?" she asks as she lays back.

"One hundred."

"Hmm."

"Where do you reckon he is?" I ask.

"Getting drunk somewhere."

"Ring Cameron again." I throw my phone at her.

She picks it up and dials his number, putting it on speaker. Cameron and Adrian have been out looking for him since about ten.

He picks up. "Hey." The music is loud and thumping through the phone. "I just found him."

I put my hand on my heart in relief. "Is he ok?" I ask shakily.

"He's at a strip club."

"What?" I gasp. Holy fuck, he's a dead man.

Bridget's eyes bulge, and she puts her hand over her mouth as she smirks.

"Are you kidding me?" I yell at Cameron through the phone.

"Shut up!" he snaps. "So, you can secretly go visit killers in prison and he can't go to a fucking strip club? Pull your head in."

"He's having a fucking baby!" I yell in an outrage.

"Last time I looked, so were you," he hits back. God, his loyalty to his brother is so fucking annoying. "I will text you the address, come and get him." He hangs up.

I hang up the phone with such force I nearly crack the glass screen.

"How fucking dare he?" I growl.

Bridget bites her bottom lip to stifle a smile.

I stand and storm into my bedroom and yank on my clothes. "Hurry up," I yell.

"I'm in my pyjamas," she calls.

"Get dressed then," I tell her.

I pull on my cardigan. "So help me God, if he's so much looked at one fucking stripper, I am going to kill him with my bare hands."

"Great," Bridget replies, deadpan. "Sounds fun."

"This isn't funny, Bridget."

"Who's laughing?" she replies dryly.

Half an hour later we walk into a small strip club with five guards following us. Max hasn't commented and I know they are loving the return of the vamped up Jerry Springer. My eyes scan the room. A small stage sits in the middle of a 'U' shaped room and a girl is dancing around a pole, writhing around on the floor wearing a g-banger. The waitresses are all topless and the way I'm feeling, all mumsy at the moment with even a cockroach in lingerie seeming sexier than me, I feel my jealousy rise.

"I swear to God, if I see so much as a neck crack he's going to die a slow, painful and bloody death."

"What are you going to do when we find him?"

"I don't know," I answer as my eyes drift around. "I'm a donkey on the edge. Anything is possible."

"Yeah, I'm kind of picking up on that." She frowns.

Our eyes continue to scan, and then over in the corner I catch sight of Cameron talking to a waitress. In front of him, Joshua sits at the end of the bench seat drinking a beer, and Adrian is farther down from him.

Joshua's eyes are fixed on the show but I know he's not watching. He's staring into space, miles away.

I walk over to the table and drop down into the seat next to him. His eyes drift to me, then back ahead in front of him.

"Go home, Natasha." He sighs.

"No."

He continues to ignore me.

I put my hand on his forearm and he shrugs it off. "Don't touch me."

"I needed to know what happened to me, Joshua, and I knew you wouldn't let me go."

His cold eyes hold mine and he tips his head back and drinks his beer.

"Baby, I needed to do this for me."

"What about what I need?"

I grab his hand on the table. "What do you need?"

"You know damn well what I need." He spits angrily.

"Joshua," I whisper.

"I need to know you are safe. This isn't just about you any-more, Natasha. I'm sick of your selfish fucking attitude."

I pick up his hand and kiss the back of it. His eyes stay down and guilt fills me. I hurt him today. I grab his hand and cup it around my cheek as I tear up.

"I love you," I whisper.

"Doesn't feel like it."

I hold my head to the side. "I do. You know I do. Please let's go home and talk about it."

"No."

"Why did you walk out on our argument today? You should have stayed and talked it through with me."

His eyes hold mine. "You don't want to know."

What's that supposed to mean? "Yes I do."

"I was so angry that I didn't trust myself to be near you."

I frown. "Why?"

He puts his head back and drinks his beer as he thinks. "Maybe I'm more like James Brennan than we all realise."

My heart drops. "Joshua." I sigh. "You would never hurt me and I know that for a fact. You would never lose control."

His haunted eyes hold mine.

"You proved that to yourself by leaving. Don't beat yourself up because you were furious with me. You had a very good reason to be angry."

He takes another swig of his beer.

"Joshua, I was off the boat in ten minutes, the guards were still awake. There was no way you could remember a thing, nobody expected something to happen when everyone was around."

He frowns. "He told you that?"

I nod and his face falls. He needs to know he couldn't have stopped it.

The girl on stage starts to moan into the microphone as she gives it to herself with a vibrator, and I hear Bridget and Adrian laugh in horror. I put my hands over the front of my stomach. "Close your ears, baby Stanton, Daddy has us hanging out in a pussy parlour listening to fake orgasms."

Amusement flickers across Joshua's face.

"Why would you do that?" he whispers.

I shrug. "I don't know. It seemed like a good plan at the time."

"He could have upset you. Anything could have happened."

I kiss his hand. "I won't do anything like that ever again, I promise."

A topless blonde with huge boobs walks over and bends over Joshua to take his empty beer bottle on the table. She gives him a dirty smile and he raises a brow at me.

I look at her, my face straight. "Buzz off, Blondie, before I stick this bar stool up your ass," I warn her.

She pulls a face and moves along.

A trace of a smile crosses his lips. "Stick a bar stool up her ass?" he repeats.

I smirk. "It would probably fit."

He smiles into his glass and I know I've got him.

"Are you taking me home, baby daddy?"

He shakes his head in defeat. "Stop fucking with my head, Natasha."

I lean in and kiss him gently. "That's my job." I rub my hand over his short dark hair.

He frowns, his lips against my lips.

"Wives fuck up their husband's nights at strip clubs all the time," I whisper. "It's a common occurrence, Mr. Stanton. Get used to it. I will do it again."

He smiles and shakes his head to himself. "Once a show stopper, always a show stopper."

"Baby, your show starts when we get home. I'm going to make it up to you." I kiss his shoulder.

He grabs my hand as he stands. "Pregnant woman aren't supposed to be horny all the time."

I smirk. "Most pregnant women don't have a Lamborghini parked in the garage."

Five Months later.

I stand with my hands on my hips as I look around baby Stanton's nursery. I'm feeling very proud of myself. We are at Willowvale and I am just putting the last of the new furnishings in. The renovations are complete and there is now a doorway between the four adjoining bedrooms so that we can be closer to the incoming crowd.

The nursery is cream with white furnishings, cream carpet and touches of mint, finished off with taupe and mint drapes. A pair of large, cream, wing back chairs and ottomans, all in the same fabric as the drapes, sit in the corner next to the window. The room is big and spacious. Adrian and I designed it and, of course, and it looks better than anything I have ever seen in a magazine. This nursery is to die for. I'm not even going to tell you how much I have spent on this house. Baby brain is making me lose all budget sense. Either that or I am getting accustomed to having nice things. Either way, I'm totally spoilt.

The bathrooms have all been remodelled and a large entertaining pool has been put in. We will be moving back here as soon as the baby is born in approximately four weeks, so we wanted all the work done before we came here permanently. We have been coming here on Thursdays and staying most weekends throughout my pregnancy. It feels like my home now and I hate leaving on Monday mornings. I can't believe it. In four weeks I'm going to have a baby, and I don't even know what to do.

The dog barks and I look out the window to see my man come up from the stables from his morning ride. I smile to myself. Those jodhpurs will be the very death of me. I have truly been adored by Joshua throughout this pregnancy. Actually, no. I have been worshiped throughout this pregnancy. Joshua cannot get enough of me and we are so physically in tune with each other, it's frightening. I'm heavily pregnant – huge – and at a time when I imagined feeling fat and frumpy, Joshua is making me feel like the most beautiful woman on the planet. How did I ever get so lucky to have a man like him love me with everything that he is?

He walks to the door and peers in. He's wet, covered in perspiration in his riding gear, and he looks edible.

"Hello, my beautiful Presh."

I smile. "Do you like it?" I hold my hand out at the bedspread I have just put in the cot.

He smiles warmly. "I do."

"How was your ride?"

He takes me in his arms and kisses me tenderly. "My first ride was ok."

"Just ok?" I whisper as his lips drop to my neck.

"My second ride will be much better." His hands roam lovingly across my stomach.

"Are you insinuating I'm a horse?" I ask in mock horror.

"No, I'm insinuating I need you naked in my bed."

"You're a sex maniac. You do know that, right?"

He smiles and bends to kiss my stomach. "How could I not be when you look like this?"

He smiles up at me as he kisses me while on his knees, and I rub my hand over the back of his head.

"How do I look?"

"You're curvy and round and constantly fucking wet for me. I could come just by looking at you at the moment. Never have I been so visually aroused in my life as I am now."

His lips take my nipple in his mouth through my flannelette pyjamas.

"I'm only going to be pregnant for four more weeks, Joshua." I smile as my eyes close in pleasure.

"I might keep you permanently pregnant."

I giggle and he stands to lead me into our bedroom where he lays me down on the bed and props me up on pillows before he takes my pyjamas off me. He spreads my legs open.

He takes my hand and kisses it and then puts my two fingers in his mouth and sucks on them as he takes my hand and puts it between my legs. "Warm yourself up for me while I shower."

His eyes darken as he pushes my two fingers into my body and back out slowly. My eyes close. God, he's so fucking hot.

"Deeper," he whispers. "I want to see it faster."

I start to pick up the pace and I feel myself moisten as I slide in easily.

"Oh, fuck, yeah." He groans.

My eyes drop to the large erection I can see through those jodhpurs and he rearranges himself.

"Shower," I murmur.

He frowns as his eyes stay fixed on my disappearing fingers.

"Does that feel good?" he whispers.

"Not as good as your cock's going to feel. Hurry up."

He hisses in approval and jumps from the bed and I hear the shower turn on. One minute later I hear it turn off and I smile. He walks back into the room as he dries himself, then drops to his knees at the side of the bed.

"I need me some clarity, baby."

Hmm, my eyes close as his mouth takes me with slow gentle adoring licks. He can't get enough of the taste of me, of the feel of me and I can't get close enough to him. I need him wrapped around me, inside of me.

"I need you," I whisper.

"Not yet. I need this." His tongue starts to lick me long and hard and my hand instinctively grips the back of his head. "Come.

I want you to come on my tongue. I need you soft and open, Presh." He continues his onslaught for ten heavenly minutes.

He nips my clitoris with his teeth and when I jump, he starts to suck me and I fall into an orgasm so strong that I lurch off the bed.

"Hmm." He groans as he tastes my orgasm. "You taste so good."

Oh dear God, this man is divine.

He stops and kisses my inner thigh as his eyes hold mine. "How do you want me?" he whispers.

I smile. Since I have been pregnant, I have been in control of our positions. I always choose how I want it as he doesn't want to pressure me into something that might hurt me.

I place my hand on his cheek. "I want to kiss you. I want to hold you."

He turns his head and kisses the palm of my hand and gently lies behind me, putting his bottom arm underneath my head. We kiss, slow and tenderly as he lifts my top leg and places my foot onto his top thigh. He spreads me with his fingers and slowly slides himself deep into my body.

We both close our eyes at the feeling. His hand drops to my round stomach and he holds it. It's like a little love cacoon. I feel so safe, so loved. He withdraws slowly and then pushes back in to me as he kisses me over my shoulder.

"You feel so good," he whispers as his hips pump me on auto-pilot. The feel of his lips on mine, his large cock inside of my body and his hand protectively on my stomach is too much. I start to quiver and he holds me tight and picks up the pace, his hand never leaving my stomach.

"You fuck me so good, baby," he breathes.

The sound of my arousal slaps heavily in the air as his body leaves and re-enters. For ten blissful minutes we writhe together, giving and taking the pleasure we both desperately need.

"I can't last." He pushes out as his lips start to quiver against mine. I clench and burst into an orgasm, and he brings his hand onto my hip and pulls me deep onto his cock so I can feel the telling jerk of his orgasm. His hand leaves my stomach and comes to my cheek and he holds me as he looks at me lovingly.

"I fucking adore you," he whispers.

I smile as my eyes glaze over. This is how lovemaking is done. "'That's good, because I fucking love you."

"Do you want a coffee?" Cameron asks.

"Tea, please," I reply.

"Hot chocolate, thanks," Didge mutters as she swipes through her phone. We are sitting on the bonnet of our car watching Joshua play Polo. Its Sunday afternoon and Bridget and Cameron have met me here. We came straight from Willowvale, and this is his last game for a while. Joshua has told them he is unavailable until after the baby is born in four weeks. I told him I'm going to go overdue, but he doesn't believe me. Adrian is working, apparently he is snowed under and couldn't make it. I need to go to the bathroom but it's such a fucking drama. I need to drag four frigging guards with me and they all wait outside while I go. Paparazzi are everywhere and I can almost feel the lenses clicking on me. This is the only place they can get their photographs of Joshua and I together and, naturally, we are being hounded because of the impending birth story. Adrian has had his styling job upped to a whole new level of Hell, Nothing bloody fits me. He is coming over weekly now and making me try stuff on, taking photos of every outfit with his phone. He then studies it so he can direct me what to wear when I'm going to be photographed, so thank Heaven for him. He makes me look better than I do. Today, I am wearing camel coloured jeans and a white linen shirt, which hangs down, with short brown boots and a brown hat that lets my hair fall out and full. My standard chunky bangles are on to hide my horrible scar. As soon as I have the baby, I'm going to see about getting some laser or something on it. I want it gone from my life.

I look at the bathrooms on the other side of the field and then over to my guards sitting on the car behind me. God, its so annoying taking guards everywhere I go.

"I need to go to the bloody bathroom again," I mutter.

"Again?" Bridget frowns.

"I know, right? Baby Stanton is sitting on something." I sigh, unimpressed.

She smiles, rubs my stomach and goes back to her phone. I try to hold it, but I really do need to go.

"I'm going to the bathroom before Cam gets back."

"Want me to come?" she asks without looking up.

"No. It's ok." I stand and wave to Max and he comes straight over. "I need to go to the bathroom."

"Ok, sure." He turns and signals to the other guards. I then drop my head and walk to the bathroom with two men in front of me, and two trailing behind. This really is over kill but it's not even worth fighting with Joshua over it. I can hear the cameras clicking as I walk. God, I must look like a beached whale. Who on Earth would want to see these photos? I get to the bathroom and join the queue to find two women before me. The light is blown so there is only light coming in from the small windows up above the sink. And then I feel it, hot and running down my leg. My eyes widen. Holy fuck, I must be wetting myself. I try to stop it but I can't and it keeps coming.

Oh my God.

Oh my fucking God.

The lady in front finishes and I duck into the stall and look down at myself. My jeans have huge wet patches running down my inside legs. Holy shit. Its still coming, so I rip down my pants and sit down but it doesn't stop. Holy crap. I've hit the bottom of the barrel. I've wet myself in public with fucking paparazzi outside waiting for the shot.

Only me, this shit could only happen to me.

I shake my hands in horror. What the hell am I going to do? I stand to look down at myself and the inside of both legs is wet right to my feet.

Oh. My. Fucking. God.

What will I do, what will I do?

I text Bridget.

**Don't say anything to Cameron
OMFG get to the bathroom
We have a fucking disaster**

She immediately texts back.

Huh?

I write back.

Just get here now!!!!!!!

She writes back.

On my way, drama queen

I stand in the stall with my hands over my mouth. I'm blushing just thinking about getting out of here.

"Hello.," I hear Bridget's voice and I open the door and peek around.

"Get in here." I grab her jumper and pull her into the cubicle with me, thankful nobody else is in the toilets.

"What are you doing, you fruitcake?"

"Look at this." I snap as I point at my pants.

Her face drops in horror. "What the hell happened?"

"I wet myself," I whisper angrily.

Her mouth drops open in horror and then she starts to giggle. "Oh my God. Funny shit."

"This is not funny shit," I gasp, outraged.

She puts her hands over her mouth. "What are we going to do?" She bends down to my stomach and points at it. "Naughty baby." She whispers.

I put my hands on my hips and throw my head back in disgust.

"It has to be a boy." She smirks. "Only a boy would do this."

"Not helping," I groan.

She stands and thinks for a moment. "I will just go out and get Max to bring the car around."

I look at her for a moment as I think. "But they will photograph my piss pants and it will be on every magazine cover tomorrow."

She screws up her face. "Yeah, I guess."

She gets out her phone and texts someone.

"Who are you texting?" I frown.

"Cameron."

"I don't want Cameron to know," I stammer in a panic.

"Cameron's a doctor, you fool. He sees people shit themselves all the time."

I throw my hands over my face in shame. "This is abysmal," I whisper.

She texts Cameron.

Mayday, mayday
Natasha has wet her pants
And we are stuck in the toilet.

We wait for a moment. "I wish Adrian was here." I whisper in mortification.

He finally texts back.

What?

Bridget texts back.

She has wet her pants and now her jeans are soaked
What do we do?

We wait for a moment and no reply. "What's he fucking doing?" Bridget snaps. "This is an emergency." She bites her bottom lip to stifle her smile and I look at her helplessly.

"You have to admit… this is pretty damn funny." She smiles.

"Fucking hilarious," I mutter dryly.

"Hello?" I hear Cameron's voice. Oh shit, he's in the girl's toilets.

I open the cubicle and pull him in. The three of us are like sardines all squashed in here. He looks down at me in horror. "Did you feel like you were wetting yourself and couldn't stop it?" he asks.

I shake my head. "No. I just felt hot wet on my legs. I'm going to die of embarrassment. Get Joshua." I admit defeat as I hold my hands over my face.

We hear a woman come into the toilets and we all stay silent. Cameron punches Bridget as she tries to hold in her giggles. The intruder eventually leaves.

My phone beeps a text from Max.

What's going on?
Why is Cameron in there?

Oh, man, this is horrific. I have to tell him. I text back.

Don't tell anyone but I have wet my pants.

He texts back.

I will bring the car around

I reply.

Yes, please.

Cameron narrows his eyes as he thinks. "Tash, I don't think you have wet yourself."

I frown.

"What are you talking about?" Bridget snaps. "What does it look like she has done, you fool?"

"It's probably amniotic fluid. I think your water has broken."

My eyes widen. "Its too early."

Bridget gasps and then bends to my stomach and points at it. "Naughty baby, stay in there. You are not cooked yet."

"Stop calling my baby naughty," I warn her as I slap her over the back of the head as she bends down.

"Well, he is," she says.

I hold my hands up in horror. "Get Joshua. Get Joshua... now."

Cameron looks at his watch. "There is only seven minutes left in the game, if you pull him off the paps will be onto you and you will be hounded all the way to the hospital."

"True," Bridget answers.

My phone beeps a text and I read it out. Its Max again.

Swap pants with Bridget to get to the car.

Bridget's face drops. "Ewww, I'm not wearing your amniotic festy fucking pants."

I start to rip my jeans down and Cameron frowns at the show that is unfolding. "Please, Bridget," I beg.

"Oh my God," she grumbles, mortified. "Cameron, do something," she whispers.

"I don't fit into her fucking jeans," he replies.

Another text comes through from Max.

Right, at the door

And I hear the cars engine. I pull my pants back up. "Let's make a run for it."

We come out of the cubicle. Cameron grabs my hand and we burst out of the bathroom into the open car door that Max is holding for me. He slams the door shut. "Oh, God, what if they got a shot of my wet pants," I cry to Cameron.

"Joshua will sue," he mutters, distracted. Max gets in the front seat and Bridget jumps in next to him.

We drive back around to the other side of the venue to where Joshua is just coming off the field. Cameron jumps out of the car and runs over to him, Joshua listens and then his eyes look up to me in the car. I see a flicker of anxiety as he tries to act calm and nods. He holds up a finger to me. Then he walks Jasper to his strapper, says something, and then comes back over to the car, jumping in the back.

"Its too early," he pants. Cameron jumps in the other side of him.

I nod. "I know, it's not due for another month."

Max dials the other security.

"Where to?" The guard asks casually.

"L.A. Memorial Hospital."

CHAPTER 10

I SIT NERVOUSLY IN the back seat of the car with Joshua's hand on my leg. Bridget sporadically looks back to check on me, while Cameron is on his phone looking something up. I think he's Googling what development stage the baby will be at. I close my eyes. It isn't time. I'm not ready, I don't even have my hospital bag packed.

I take out my phone to text Mum and Abbie.

Disaster.
Wet my pants at polo.
Cameron thinks my water have broken.
On the way to hospital, keep you posted.

Damn it, Mum arrives in two weeks for the birth. I really wanted her here. You really are a naughty baby.

I start to dial a number. "Who are you ringing?" Joshua asks.

"I need to ring Adrian."

"What for?"

"I don't have anything with me," I tell him in a panic.

He raises a brow but wisely holds his tongue as I switch it onto speaker.

"Hey, baby," Adrian answers.

"Oh my God, Adrian. I'm having a nightmare," I cry.

"What is it?"

"I wet my pants at polo and now Cameron thinks that it's amniotic fluid and we are on our way to the hospital."

"But… you are not due for another twenty-nine days."

I smile. Of course he would know the exact days. "I know. What if they got a shot of me with wet pants?"

Joshua rolls his eyes. "Who cares?" he interjects. "We got bigger fucking problems."

Adrian pauses as he thinks. "That's ok, we will just issue a statement saying the images were photoshopped."

"You could do that?" I ask hopefully.

"Of course we can. Swing past home and get changed and then go to the hospital."

"Ok." I nod. Good thinking.

"No!" Cameron snaps. "We need to get to the hospital as a matter of urgency and stop this labour."

Joshua's worried eyes flick to Cameron. "What's the problem with this early."

"The baby's lungs are still developing and it may have trouble breathing."

My face falls and Bridget reaches over the seat and grabs my hand. "Tash, this is just a false alarm. Everybody has false alarm stories, don't they Cameron?" She glares at him in a *shut the fuck up, your scaring her* look.

"Yes, yes, of course," Cameron corrects himself.

I think for a moment. "Adrian, can you go to our house and pack me a bag, please?"

"Of course, baby."

I think for a moment. "Can you get my pink dressing gown and my nightdress from the bathroom?"

"Yes, what else?"

"Umm." I think for a moment, what else do I need? Bridget can go and get my personal stuff later. My eyes glance at Joshua in his Polo gear. "Can you grab Joshua some clothes, too?"

"Ok, I will meet you there."

"Thank you."

Joshua grabs my hand again and winks.

I feel sick to my stomach. What if something goes wrong? What if the baby is underdeveloped?

"It will be ok, Presh," Joshua saysassures me softly.

I nod nervously and put my head onto his shoulder. He wraps his arm around me. I rub my large stomach. Please behave in there and stop trying to escape. I'm not ready and neither are you.

After the slowest drive in history, we finally get to the hospital and find two nurses waiting at the door with a gown. They come over to the car and pass it in. "Put this on, dear."

I take it with thanks and put it over my clothes. No doubt Adrian has rang ahead and organised this.

I waddle my way through the hospital with Joshua, Bridget and Cameron until we get to the maternity ward. The young nurse on the desk sees us and her face drops in shock.

"O-oh," she stutters before regaining composure. "I mean… Hello. Can I help you?" She's obviously a Joshua fan.

Joshua glares at her.

"Mrs. Stanton needs to see her doctor. Page Dr. Walton immediately!" Cameron snaps.

"Yes, sir."

An elderly, kind midwife comes out and smiles. "Hello, my dear, my name is Nancy. What's going on here?"

Cameron goes to interject and she holds her hand up to stop him.

"I'm talking to?" She raises her eyebrows at him in question.

"Natasha," I murmur softly.

"I'm a doctor," Cameron states, annoyed that he has just been dismissed.

She smiles warmly and takes my hand. I bite my bottom lip to stifle my smile. These older midwifes obviously don't take shit from young doctors. She doesn't give a damn who he is.

"Hello, Natasha. Why are you here, my dear?"

"Um." I swallow my nerves. "I think my waters may have broken but it is too early."

"How far along are you?"

"Thirty-six weeks."

She smiles calmly. "I see." Oh, this midwife is good, really good. She looks between Cameron and Joshua. "And who is the father?"

"Me," Joshua snaps, affronted that there could be any doubt.

She smiles again. "And what is your name?"

Bridget and I exchange looks. She doesn't know who we are. Thank God for that.

"Joshua," he replies.

"And this is your family?" She looks between Bridget and Cameron, and they both nod.

"Ok, lets take you through here with Joshua to run some tests. Your family can wait in the waiting room."

Cameron and Bridget wave us off nervously and take a seat in the waiting room.

Nancy leads us into a hospital room and opens the bathroom door to the side. "Just go into the bathroom, dear, and remove your clothes and underwear, then put this gown on." She retrieves a gown from the cupboard and passes it to me. I nod nervously and do as she instructed. I put it on and take my place on the bed. She wheels a trolley in and attaches pads that are hooked up to monitor, to my stomach. The baby's heartbeat starts to bleep a little noise. "Ah, there it is. A beautiful strong little heartbeat." Nancy smiles.

My relieved eyes turn to focus on Joshua, and he smiles his first smile in two hours, squeezing my hand.

"The doctor is on his way and he will inspect you when he gets here."

"Ok," I murmur.

"Here is the buzzer." She hands me a control thingy from above the bed. "If you need anything, just call me."

We both smile. "Thank you." She leaves the room.

Joshua and I sit for what seems like forever. Joshua is silent and pensive as he sits in the chair next to the bed.

I look around the room nervously. "This isn't like the rooms we inspected, is it?"

"Hmm." Joshua groans deep in thought.

"We don't have a spa bath. I thought we were supposed to have a spa bath?"

"Hmm." Joshua repeats, as he stands and starts to pace at the end of the bed.

"Do you think we will get in the spa?"

He doesn't answer me, instead running his hands through his hair nervously.

"Are you listening to me?"

"Hmm."

We hear a commotion down the hall and someone crying.

Joshua's face falls and he goes pale.

"Wonder what's going on down there?" I whisper. "Go and see."

Joshua frowns. "What?"

"Open the door and see who is crying. I want to know if it's a mother giving birth."

"Oh, for fucks sake, I'm not doing that. Mind your own business!" he snaps in frustration.

We hear Nancy's calm voice. "Come back into the room, dear, its ok."

We hear more tears and a door slam.

I tap my foot on the bed impatiently as Joshua sits back in his chair. He rubs his index finger back and forth across his lips in his classic thinking pose. He is silently freaking out.

The room is quiet and still. "This is boring, isn't it?" I mutter.

Joshua blows out a breath and rolls his eyes.

"Do you think I'm in labour?" I ask.

"Natasha" He sighs.

I smile cheekily. "Yes, my Lamborghini?"

"Why don't you have a sleep? This is going to be a very long day if you don't relax.'"

I screw up my face. "As if I could sleep." I continue to tap my foot in excitement as I sit in my bed and look around.

He scratches the back of his head in frustration. I know he wants to snap at me and say 'shut up, I'm thinking' but he's holding his tongue.

"Have you eaten?" he asks.

"No, I'm good."

"Are you hungry?"

"Nope."

"You will need your strength later."

"I know," I reply casually.

"Close your eyes and rest, Presh." He rubs his hand on my thigh.

I smile mischievously. I'm going to play with him a bit. "Maybe we should have sex, Joshua. That would be cool, right? And it would take my mind off things?"

His face falls in horror. "Natasha. That is the absolute furthest thing from my mind, and *you* have just cemented what I always thought."

I smile broadly. "And what did you always think?"

"You are a bona fide sex maniac."

I raise my eyebrows. "Takes one to know one. I learnt from the best."

Joshua closes his eyes and pinches the bridge of his nose. God, it's so fun annoying him when he's so stressed out.

After an extended time, Dr. Walton walks in with a nurse. "Hello, Joshua and Natasha." He smiles calmly.

Joshua stands and shakes his hand. "Hello."

"Hi," I say through a smile.

He starts to read the printout from the monitor attached to my stomach. He smiles. "This is a bit earlier than we expected, isn't it?"

"Yes." I nod.

Joshua holds his breath. I'm expecting him to turn blue at any moment.

"I'm just going to examine you." He pulls on a pair of gloves. "Pull your legs back, Natasha."

He pulls my gown up around my waist.

Joshua cringes and drops his head, openly freaking out now.

"I'm alright, Joshua." I smile as I hold my hand out for him.

He nods once. That was his *shut up* nod.

The doctor puts lube on his hand and goes in, feeling around, while both Joshua and I hold our breaths.

He smiles broadly and takes off his gloves. "Well, my dear, your water has broken."

"Oh," I mutter, I really did think it was a false alarm.

Joshua frowns. "Isn't it too early? Can we stop it?"

"No, it will be ok. Once the amniotic fluid is lost, we need to go to the birth plan."

I frown. Shit.

"The baby is relatively big, so I can't see any problems with it at this stage. It's actually more dangerous to delay."

"Ok." I nod.

"Now you have two options." The Dr. continues.

"What?" Joshua asks too quickly.

"You haven't had any contractions yet, have you?"

I shake my head. "No."

"Well, we can either wait for you to go into labour naturally, which may take a while, seeing how you are this early."

"How long is a while?" Joshua frowns.

He shrugs. "Hard to say, but you are not dilated at all, so I would assume up to twelve hours."

Joshua's face falls in horror. "Twelve hours before she even goes into labour?"

"Yes."

"What's the other option?" Joshua asks as his eyes flick to mine.

"We could put you on a drip and speed up the process."

"Induce me?" I ask.

"Yes."

My eyes hold Joshua's, and the worry on his poor face makes my decision. I want this done. I want our baby in our arms.

"I would like to be induced, please, if you are sure that's ok for the baby?"

"Yes, of course." Dr. Walton smiles.

Joshua swallows the lump in his throat, he looks like he is going to throw up, and he's telling me to calm down and relax?

Dr. Walton turns to the nurse. "Please transfer Natasha to a birthing suite and arrange an induction."

"Yes, Doctor." She smiles.

He turns back to me. "Now, Natasha, I know you have discussed with me your pain relief."

"I don't want any," I reply.

Joshua closes his eyes.

"Induction is faster and stronger. I would suggest you don't dismiss it completely. The anaesthetist is here and can perform an epidural."

"No, thanks." I force a smile. No fucker is putting a needle in my spine. I have heard the horror stories.

Joshua runs his hands nervously through his hair again.

Dr. Walton smiles warmly. "I am going home for a few hours and I will be back to check on you."

"Ah, no!" Joshua snaps. "I want you here the whole time."

The doctor smiles warmly. "Joshua, it's fine. I live around the corner and it won't be instantaneous. We have time and I will be here for most of the night. I have another patient also in labour down the hall."

"What time will you be back?" Joshua snaps.

"I will be back at about eight for the rest of the night. You need to relax, this is a natural process and you being stressed won't help anyone. Least not your wife."

Joshua's worried eyes flick to mine. I smile softly and hold my hand out for him. "It's ok, baby," I whisper.

He nods nervously. "Ok."

The doctor leaves and the nurse smiles warmly. "We are going down to the birthing suite now. Do you have a bag with you?"

"My friend has it in the waiting room."

She smiles. "Go and get your bag and come back to me at the desk and we will go into the birthing suite."

I swallow my nerves. "Ok," I whisper.

She leaves the room and Joshua grabs me into an embrace so tight I can hardly breathe.

I whisper into the top of his head, "Relax."

"I don't like this," he breathes.

"Joshua. Aren't you supposed to be the strong one here?" I gently kiss him.

His worried eyes hold mine and I cup his cheek in my hand.

"We got this, baby," I whisper.

"I don't like this," he repeats softly.

"I know you don't but it *is* going to be ok."

He nods and helps me down from the bed, and we make our way to the waiting room.

Cameron is pacing, Adrian is standing and Bridget is sitting. They all rush over to us.

"Oh my God," Adrian splutters. "What's going on?"

"I'm getting induced."

"Fuck." Bridget stammers as her face falls. "That shit is supposed to hurt."

"Shut the hell up," Joshua snaps.

Cameron slaps Joshua on the back. "Get ready for a ride, old boy. You are about to see vaginas in a whole new stretching light."

Bridget and I giggle, and the blood drains from Joshua's face.

"That's not funny, Cameron," Adrian spits. "You're going to be fine, baby. You are the toughest chick I know." He wraps his large arms around me and squeezes me tight.

I smile. "I know." And it's true. I feel damn invincible at this moment in time. Bring it. Bring it the fuck on and give me my baby.

Adrian passes me my overnight bag. "I packed you both some clothes, and I put in some clothes for the baby, too."

I smile brightly. "Styling baby Stanton already?"

He throws me a wink. "Of course."

Bridget cuddles me. "Oh, Tash. I love you. Everything will be fine. I am waiting out here just in case you need me," she whispers into my hair.

I nod and feel a little bit bad that I didn't want anyone but Joshua with me at the birth. This is such a precious moment, one I only want to share with him.

Cameron wraps his arms around me. "Pain management, chick. There are no medals for bravery." He kisses me on the cheek and shakes Joshua's hand.

I nod and fake a smile. "I just want to ring Mum quickly." I dial Mum's number.

"Hello, darling," she answers, and for the first time today I feel teary. I really wanted her here.

"Hi, Mum. My water has broken and I'm being induced."

"Oh, it's going to be wonderful. Enjoy it."

I nod and feel a little better.

"I love you, darling. Good luck and ring me as soon as you can. I will sit by the phone."

"Ok." I hesitate as my eyes tear up. "I love you."

As if sensing my fear, she speaks again. "Tash, you're going to be ok. Don't be scared. Go and get your baby."

I nod with renewed purpose. "Bye, Mum." I hang up the phone and turn to the others.

"Let's do this shit," I state, and turn and walk back to reception with them all cheering me on from behind. I feel like Rocky Fucking Balboa.

We are steered down the corridor by the nurse who eventually opens a door at the end of the hall. Joshua and I walk in sheepishly; this is frigging scary. If these walls could talk, I'm sure they would have some gruesome stories.

She places four towels on the bed. "I'm sure you two would like to shower and make yourself more comfortable before we put you on the drip."

My eyes find Joshua in his dirty polo get up and I smile.

"Thank you."

He nods and seems to remember, for the first time, what he is wearing.

She leaves the room and I walk into the bathroom. "Oh, look! A spa bath."

"You can forget it," Joshua mumbles from the other room. "We are not getting in that spa bath."

I smile. He's so right, I can think of nothing worse than sitting in a bloody bath.

I shower, get into my gown, then into bed. Joshua showers and changes into new clothes and sits next to the bed, too, taking my hand. He's quiet, too quiet.

The nurse comes in, places the cannula in the back of my hand and puts the medication into the drip. My heartbeat is pumping so damn hard, it will be a miracle if I don't have a heart attack before the birth even begins. She hooks me back up to the heart rate monitor and we, once again, hear the magic of our baby's heartbeat.

She eventually leaves, and Joshua blows out a relieved breath as he takes my hand and kisses the back of it.

"Now we wait," he whispers.

I smile. "Are we sure about the names?" I ask.

His face falls. "Don't you like them anymore?"

"Yes, it would help if it didn't know so many people. It's annoying." I sigh.

Joshua bites his bottom lip to contain his smile. One of his prerequisites is that he doesn't know anyone with the same name. Do you know how hard that is? He knows one of everything.

The door opens and a tall young man walks in. "Hello." He shakes our hands. "I'm Jeremy Seymour. I'm the resident anaesthetist."

"Hello."

"I just wanted to go through an epidural with you."

"No, I'm fine, thanks," I reply. Bloody hell, they really do try and force this shit down your throat.

He smiles warmly. "That's fine. I just want you to know that there is only a small window where you can have it, and once that has passed, it's too late."

I nod. "Thank you. I am really focused on doing this naturally."

The doctor smiles warmly. "Of course. Good luck."

The doctor leaves us in peace.

Josh takes my hand. "'Tash, they all keep going on about this, maybe you should do it. Like Cam said, there is no bravery medal at the end."

I smile. "Josh, I am stronger than you think."

"I know," he admits nervously.

"Trust me. I can do this."

Seven hours later

"Ahhhhh, Get me a fucking epidural. Get it to me *now*!" I scream as I writhe around in pain on the bed. Joshua is wet with perspiration and has thrown up four times just from stress. This isn't childbirth of natural free love and all that glow. This is an exorcism of The Devil, where he is ripping himself out of my body.

I shake my head at Joshua frantically. "No. No. Take me home, Josh. Take me home. Take me home. Take me home."

"Baby," Joshua whispers. "Calm down."

"It is not oh fucking kaaaay!" I scream.

"Natasha."

"I don't want a baby anymore. I don't want a baby anymore. You have it," I whisper frantically. I'm wet with perspiration and the tears are running down my face. Holy fucking shit. This hurts. Like murdering death pain, hurts.

"I want an epidural. Get that guy back. Get him back." I point to the door and start to panic as I feel another contraction coming.

I screw up my face and clench. "Ahhhh!" I cry as I curl up in a ball.

"This is ridiculous," Joshua cries. "Get her an epidural now!"

"Too late, Joshua," Dr. Walton tells him. "She's nine centimetres dilated. Almost time to push."

Joshua's wide eyes meet mine. Oh dear God. I'm going to die. I am going to die today.

I start to shake my head. "No, no, no."

Dr. Walton smiles calmly.

My frantic eyes meet Joshua's again. "I can't do this, Josh," I sob. "This is too hard. I can't do it. Knock me out, give me a C-section."

Joshua's eyes dart from mine to the doctor's in panic.

"I want to go to the bathroom," I announce.

Joshua raises his eyebrows in question and I nod. "Yes, I want to go."

"No, Natasha, you have to stay in bed at this stage," Dr. Walton replies. "If you need to go, we will get you a bed pan." I scowl. Oh, this is horrible.

I'm beside myself. I don't think I can do this. I'm crying uncontrollably.

Joshua looks to the doctor and nurse in the room. "Can you give us a moment alone, please?"

"Of course."

I watch as they both leave the room.

Joshua bends and kisses my head.

"Presh, please don't cry."

"Josh," I whisper. "I can't do this." The tears run freely down my face. "Please get them to C-section me."

Joshua grabs my face. "You listen to me." His voice is calm and assertive.

My scared eyes search his.

"If I could have this baby for us, you know that I would."

The tears run down my face.

"You have got this, Natasha."

I stare at him as my heart races and, for some reason, the past comes flashing through my mind. I see the handsome nineteen-year-old university student who loved me with all of his heart. Then I see the dominant man I met seven years later.

"You can do this," whispers my controlled and devoted husband.

I drop my head. We have been through so much, so much pain to be together and yet here I am in the pinnacle of our relationship, and I am crumbling like a flake.

"I know you can do this. Be the brave woman I know that you are," Joshua whispers. His eyes are full of fear, but more than that, I can see love. He loves me so much.

"Josh," I whisper through my fear.

He puts his finger to my lip to quieten me. "Remember what we learned in birthing class."

I nod.

He kisses me tenderly and his tongues sweeps through my open lips.

He pulls my hair back aggressively so that I have to look in his eyes and, like a miracle, the dominant gesture he usually saves for our bedroom instantly eases my panic.

"I love you," he whispers and I smile through my tears. "Bring me our child."

Goosebumps scatter over my skin and I nod.

"Without hesitation, without fear, give birth to our baby."

I smile as my tears flow. He's right, there is no easy way to do this. Nobody else can do this for us. It's up to me and me alone.

I need to get myself together.

"I love you," I whisper.

"I know you can do this." He kisses me again and I taste my salty tears on my lips.

"Don't be scared," he whispers.

"I'm not," I assure him with renewed purpose. "I will."

And as if the heavens have opened up, I now have clarity. I can see the end. I want our baby.

Joshua goes to the door and calls the doctor back in.

I close my eyes and ride through the next contraction in silence. Dr. Walton checks me again.

"Natasha, on the next contraction, I want you to push."

I nod, close my eyes and wait until the contraction comes.

"Now, Natasha, push now."

Joshua

I am at Natasha's side holding her hand. She closes her eyes and she pushes. She pushes with everything that she has and, as if by some miracle, our baby's head appears. Oh dear God. I stay next to my love and don't have time to think. The next contraction comes almost immediately and she pushes again.

"That's is, baby," I whisper appreciatively. For fifteen minutes she continues to push.

"You are going great, Presh," I chant. "Keep going, baby."

I feel like I am having an out of body experience. I'm in my own private world watching this from above and I'm terrified.

The contraction comes. She pushes again and finally, I see the baby slide into the doctor's hands.

I grab Natasha into an embrace and she cries in relief. "You did it, Presh. You did it."

"Joshua, come and cut the cord," Dr, Walton instructs.

My heart hammers in my chest and I hold the scissors with shaky hands to cut the umbilical cord. I grab Tash in an embrace again, I can't believe this is happening.

Tash half laughs and half cries and we both look toward the baby and hear a loud scream.

I smile, as I am overcome with emotion

"It's a little girl." Dr. Walton smiles warmly.

"A girl?" I whisper in wonder. We didn't want to know the sex before the birth.

The nurse wraps her in a blanket and immediately weighs her. "Six pounds, which is a good size for an early baby." She smiles.

I stand completely entranced as I watch the tiny girl in the nurse's arms. She wraps her in a pink blanket and hands her to me.

My heart stops.

This baby, this tiny piece of Natasha and me... I have no words as the overwhelming feeling of love infiltrates every cell in my body. My eyes fall to my girl in bed. Natasha is dishevelled and wet with perspiration but she has never looked more beautiful.

I carefully lay the precious little bundle onto her mother's chest.

I grab Natasha and hold her tight. "I love you," I whisper into her hair. "I love you, I love you," I repeat as I squeeze her.

"I love you too, baby," she whispers through tears. She gently kisses her daughter's forehead and rearranges her gently so that we can look at her. She's tiny, with blue eyes and a scattering of fair hair.

Is this real?

Is this our baby?

As if in the twilight zone, this perfect little pink person stares up at me.

"Joshua," Natasha whispers through tears.

I shake my head in disbelief, unable to speak.

The doctor checks Natasha. "I need to do a little repair work here, Natasha."

I stand concerned. "What's wrong?" I frown.

"She needs some stitches."

My face falls. "Oh."

"That's ok," she whispers as she grabs my hand to reassure me.

"Take your daughter, Joshua," the doctor instructs.

My face falls and I fumble. I don't know how to hold this tiny thing without hurting her, but I lift her into my arms and sit in the chair next to the bed and stare at the little girl in my arms.

She's tiny, so tiny and so perfect. My eyes float up to Natasha. "Are you ok, Presh?" I ask. God, I hate that she has had to go through so much today.

The doctor gives her an injection and she smiles sleepily as she nods. "I'm ok, Josh."

My eyes fall back to the little person in my arms and I frown, unwrapping a little of her blanket to look at her, and as if by some miracle, she reaches out and wraps her tiny hand around my pointer finger. I feel my heart somersault in my chest as every emotion overwhelms me. My eyes fill with tears and I lift her precious little hand to my mouth and kiss the back of it.

This is love in its highest form.

Tears start to run down my face

"Happy Birthday," I whisper.

I feel my heart swell with so much love, I could burst.

We did it. We did it. We made a baby.

My eyes rise back to the beautiful, brave woman who did this – the woman who brought me this happiness today. We have come so far and fought so hard and... words escape me. Never in a million years would I have thought, all those years ago when I was filling her void with other women, that this precise moment was in my future... that this higher level of being could ever be achieved.

I watch Natasha intently as our relationship hits another stratosphere.

I fucking love this woman with every ounce of my being.

"What's her name?" The doctor asks.

My eyes drop to the precious bundle in my arms. "Jordana May Stanton," I whisper.

"What a beautiful name." The doctor smiles.

"It is," I reply, totally distracted by the tiny little person in my hands.

The doctor finishes twenty minutes later, and I hand our baby back to Natasha. The nurse arranges her to try and feed. I stand still and hold my breath as I watch. She latches on and starts to suck and I feel the floor fall from underneath me. This is one of the most basic human needs, and yet it may just be the most intimate and beautiful thing I have ever seen. I watch the woman I love turn into a mother. My eyes well up again and I wipe my tears with the back of my hands.

Natasha smiles up at me with love in her eyes. "Josh." She smiles. "Look what we made?"

"I love you so much," I whisper as I sit on the bed and watch her feed our child. For half an hour, we stay silent and still as we watch our baby. I am in awe. There is nothing on Earth that could ever compare to this feeling. Natasha hands her back to me and I sit and stare at her in my arms. I know I should go outside and tell everyone the news, but I don't want to break this moment. This is time that I can never get back and they are all going to have to wait.

"Can I take a shower?" Natasha asks. "I feel like I have just fought ten rounds with Mike Tyson," she murmurs.

"Of course," the nurse replies. "I will—"

I cut the nurse off. "I will take care of Natasha."

I lay Jordana in her little wheel around crib and help Tash out of bed, and then I push the crib as I help Tash. It seems weird having two people to look after now.

"You can leave the baby here. I will watch her." The nurse smiles.

"I can take care of them both," I reply. Now more than ever, my protective instincts have kicked in. I'm not leaving either of them alone for even a minute.

I park Jordana into the corner of the bathroom and lead Tash into the shower, helping her wash the blood from her body gently.

She's so swollen and she has lots of stitches. "Oh, baby," I whisper, this is horrific. "Are you ok?"

She nods and holds me tight.

To be honest I'm feeling a little fragile myself, that whole birthing thing is other worldly.

She kisses me, and it's as though our relationship just hit a whole higher level of intimacy.

"I have never loved you more than I do today," I whisper.

We stand alone in the shower in each other's arms, selflessly blocking out the rest of the world as we kiss and celebrate the making of a perfect little girl.

Jordana May Stanton.

Four Years Later

Natasha

"Jordy why are you in different clothes?" I ask as she flits around the kitchen in a little pink ballerina costume.

"I got dirty," Little Miss replies.

I shake my head at Joshua and he smirks. This is her fourth outfit today. Jordana, A.K.A, Jordy, Jay or Jay bird, is… hmm, what's the word for it? Strong willed, just like her father.

She gives the word defiant a whole new meaning. She's super intelligent and super bossy.

We live at Willowvale now with Jordy and our other two children. Estella, who we call Ellie, is two and a half, and Blake, our son, is one. We are outnumbered. There are more little people in this house than adults and we don't stand a chance of getting out of here alive.

The beautiful mansion that I once thought was a museum is now strewn with toys, highchairs and nappy wipes. Joshua's office has *Lego* on the floor and tiny little handprints are all over the windows. Ellie waddles after Joshua and holds her hands up. He picks her up without thinking. Ellie is the only placid child we have, and Joshua says she's the only drama free person in the house. Being attracted and married to a dominant male is hot… but bringing up his two dominant children is just damn hard work. Ellie points to the walk in pantry and Joshua walks over and opens it for her. I watch them together. In fact, I watch him with all of our children. This huge, muscular man is a pussycat at the mere mention of the word daddy.

"A banana?" he asks as he holds one up.

She shakes her head. She has sandy hair that curls on the ends, and large blue eyes. She is fairer than the other two

"Yogie," her little voice tells him.

"Yoghurt?" he questions.

She smiles broadly and nods as he takes it from the fridge. He fills her a bowl and sits her in her high chair, placing everything out for her to devour.

He watches her lovingly for a moment as she spoons it into her mouth. This one has him wrapped around her little finger.

Jordy and Blake look like Joshua with darker hair and darker skin and blue eyes. They are like him in personality, too – strong willed and unmanageable. Joshua is getting payback, and I love every moment of watching him try to control them. It's a battle of the wills, constantly.

The dog barks and we hear the crunch of tyres. Jordy's eyes widen in excitement and she runs to the front of the house to peek out the window.

"Mercy is here!" she yells excitedly.

Mercy... also known as Murphy, as in Adrian Murphy.

Jordy heard the boys calling him Murphy once and couldn't say it, so she started calling him Mercy and it stuck. Now the other kids just think that's his name.

The door opens and Jordy squeals in delight and he picks her up, laughs and spins her around. Cameron is behind him and he growls like a monster, chasing them up the hall as Adrian runs with her in his arm.

"He's scary." Adrian laughs. "Hide me, Jordy. Hide me."

She laughs out loud as Cameron pretends to chase them. Jarvis follows them in, carrying a couple of suit bags. They burst into the large kitchen area. We have extended and now have another living room off the kitchen, seeing how we seem to be here all the time with the kids. Cameron swoops Blake off the floor and kisses Ellie gently on the head as she continues eating her yoghurt. The boys all dote on the children. They come to visit them weekly, not us, I'm sure of it.

Bridget is living in Australia and so is Abbie. Bridget is coming for a visit next week with Mum, not that I'm counting the days or anything. Mum lives between here and Australia. She has met a nice man from the village here who she calls her friend. Cameron is back at University to be a surgeon and Adrian is running the company for Joshua and living in L.A.

Joshua works from home for four days and in the office in L.A. on the other day. I have opened a small psychology practice in town here but I only open two days a week. Birgetta helps Joshua with the kids on those days.

Ben has returned to South Africa after he went and worked with my brother, Brock, for a while. Oh, and get this: Jesten works with my brother. There are five ex Special Forces men working together in his security company named Marx. Pretty cool, hey?

"Did you remember the dresses?" I ask Adrian.

He rolls his eyes. "Yes, that's the reason we came, isn't it?"

He puts Jordy down and she runs upstairs while Jarvis retrieves the suit bags for Adrian. I smile broadly and kiss Jarvis on the cheek as I take them from him. He has become so dear to all of us and I am beyond grateful that Joshua brought him into our lives.

Joshua stands behind me, slips his arms around my waist and kisses my temple. I smile against his lips. How did I ever get so lucky? Cameron spins Blake around and he laughs out loud.

"You are growing up, little man." He smiles broadly.

Blake puts his hands on Cameron's face and squeals with laughter and then he spots Joshua and all is forgotten in the world. He holds his arms out to him and scrunches his little hands open and closed. Joshua takes him from Cam and kisses the top of his head.

"Dad, Dad, Dad." He smiles.

Adrian opens the suit bags on the kitchen table.

"So, we have this one." He pulls out a black dress and Cameron and Joshua roll their eyes at each other. Jarvis smiles and flops onto the lounge.

"This is important!" I snap.

We have opened a charity: The Stanton Mental Health Institute, and we have our first annual ball next week. I'm speaking and I'm as nervous as hell. I have to look amazing. Nicholas is on the committee and we are following his lead from his work in Australia.

He pulls out a black gown.

"Oh, wow." I smile, and I hold it up to me. "This is gorgeous."

"It is, isn't it?" Adrian smiles. "But I think I like the pink one better."

He starts to unzip the bag but we are interrupted by Jordy.

"I'm going riding," she announces. She is wearing her full riding kit, jodhpurs, boots, a little hard hat with her two dark plaits hanging down.

Everybody smirks. What next?

"No, you are not. We already went riding this morning," Joshua tells her.

"Yes, I know. I'm going again. I need to practice to get better, Dad."

I smirk, like Joshua, Jordy is mad for horses.

"No, you are not. You can go again later," Joshua replies.

"I am. Max will take me." She heads out the back door.

"Jordana," Joshua calls after her. "Come back here now."

"No!" she yells as she marches down toward the stables.

"This fucking kid," Joshua mumbles under his breath, and we all laugh. He takes off after her and we hear them have a full stand up argument on the path.

I smirk and turn the jug on. "You want some tea, boys?" I watch Joshua and Jordy fight on the pathway. His plan for six children could be the very death of him, and he would die if he knew I suspected that I'm pregnant again.

"Yes, please."

"Jordy still whipping his ass around Willowvale?" Cameron smirks.

I smile. "Trying to."

Jordana comes marching through the door in tantrum, tears everywhere, followed by Joshua.

"You can go up to your room, thank you," Joshua says sternly.

She folds her arms in a huff. "I am going to my room," she cries. "And I'm slamming my door."

Joshua's eyes narrow. "Don't you dare."

"I am!" she yells as she storms past us.

Cameron and Adrian smile into their tea. It really is fun watching Joshua having stand up arguments with a sweet looking four-year-old girl. Most grown men don't cross him.

"I can't fucking wait until she's sixteen, man. It is going to be on like Donkey Kong." Cameron smiles.

Joshua fakes a shiver.

We all laugh. Let the games begin.

Natasha

My eyes flick over to Joshua who stands at the bar with his father, mum, Bridget, Cameron and Stephanie. Stephanie is Joshua's father's new girlfriend. She's beautiful and only four years older than Scott.

Margaret is here to support us, although the invitation didn't extend to her fiancé, James Brennan. I'm happy that she's happy, but I will never get over the lies she told. They went on for far too long. I tolerate her for the sake of my children, but who knows what the future will bring? I don't want them to see me have contempt for my mother-in-law. It's a daily struggle, one that I would walk away from if I didn't know how hard we fought to keep the family together. My eyes look around at the opulent ballroom in amazement. This is something out of this world. I am so proud of all that we have accomplished.

We are at the first Stanton Mental Health Institute charity ball and I am flitting around the room with my committee. Nicholas and I have joined forces and we make a mean team.

The voice echoes from the stage. "Can I please welcome to the stage, Natasha Stanton."

The crowd clap and I make my way through the throes of people, walking nervously up to the stage.

I take my place behind the microphone and I feel my heart swell with pride. This is what I was meant to be doing. This is my calling. I have never felt so strongly about anything as I do about being an advocate for mental health.

I am wearing a heavy lace fitted black dress and my hair is out and full. Adrian has done well with this little number. I feel confident and comfortable.

I smile nervously and give a little wave to the crowd

Everyone laughs softly, and my eyes search the crowd for my man.

"Hello. I would, once again, like to thank you all for coming tonight."

This is my second speech of the night. The first one I gave had people in tears.

"The Stanton Mental Health Institute has one goal and one goal only. To advocate, care for and create funding for research on mental health. With your help, we can break down the stigmatism and create hope and quality care."

I open the envelope and smile broadly as I read the next line. Oh my God, is this the true figure?

I look up and find Joshua in the crowd and I feel myself tear up.

"It is my great pleasure to announce that, thanks to your generosity, we have raised eleven point two million dollars tonight."

The crowd all cheer and I drop my chin to my chest to hide my emotion. The committee and everyone involved have worked so damn hard on this project. Cameron, his father and Joshua have called on every contact they know to make this a success. We are all so proud of this charity.

I can't do anything but stand and applaud along with the audience for an extended time.

I raise my hand to the committee and the crowd continues to clap.

"From all of us at the Stanton Mental Health Institute, we give you a huge thank you. Tonight's funding will change so many lives," I announce through my tears. I bow softly and the crowd clap and cheer and I exit the stage to find my man.

I arrive back with my family and smile with happiness. They are all celebrating the monetary figure.

Cameron kisses my cheek. "Fucking hell, Tash. Eleven million!" he whispers.

Dad shakes Joshua's hand aggressively. "Well done, son." He turns and kisses me. "Well done, Natasha." He smiles.

I smile again broadly as I feel lips on my cheek and a hand slide around my waist. I turn to see my handsome husband and I kiss him gently on the lips.

"Did I sound ok?" I ask.

"Perfect." He smiles. "I'm so proud of you, Presh," he whispers.

I smile and put both of my arms around his neck. "The formalities are over. Please get me a drink, my Lambo?"

He smiles and drops his hand to my behind. He cracks his neck hard as he gives me that look that he does so well.

His eyes drop to my breasts that are pushed up against his chest, and I feel his cock harden up against my body through his dinner suit.

"You just got yourself a ticket to Pound Town, Mrs. Stanton," he whispers in my ear.

My lips linger on his and his sweet scent surrounds me.

"Please," I breathe as I subtly rub my body up against his erection.

"I want the scenic route," I whisper.

He smiles broadly. "We will always take the long way, Presh."

He kisses me again.

"You know it, baby." I smirk.

I will never get enough of this man.

Of the life he has brought me.

Of the children he has given me.

Of the way he makes me feel.

As long as he loves me, there will always be magic

Thank you so, so much for reading

Find me at tlswanauthor.com

Continue in Stanton Land with my upcoming books

Marx Girl

Anastas

Dr Stanton

De Luca

Men of Marx series –Jesten and Brock

Made in the USA
Las Vegas, NV
26 November 2022

60436250R00125